*He wondered if she had only sex
on her mind*

Leah a_____all hot desire.
Stopp_____like her life
depend_____

Good _____ to him. "Hello to
you, too_____red, cupping her shoulders and
pulling her slightly away.

She grabbed his hand and started leading him into
the house, leaving no doubt about her motivations
for being there. It made him a little uneasy.

"Can a guy catch a shower first?" he asked, stalling.

She turned toward him. "But I want you to be dirty."
The flush of passion on her pale cheeks made it clear
what she meant.

J.T. swallowed hard. Just the passion in Leah's face
made him forget about the work that needed to be
done, forget that she'd very obviously come out just
for sex.

He loved claiming her sweet body. Loved making
her go over the edge.

But it was her heart he was after.

And he was afraid he'd never reach it.

Dear Reader,

SLEEPING WITH SECRETS... Intrigued? We have to admit the title of this miniseries grabbed us from the start and refused to let go. It tempted us to step into the shadows, opening our eyes to all sorts of forbidden, sexy ideas that began with our title in the January 2004 *Private Scandals* anthology and continues with three books for the Blaze line.

In the first story, *Forbidden,* sexy single mom Leah Dubois Burger had life all figured out...until J. T. West awakened a restlessness in her a year and a half ago, setting off a chain reaction that was as destructive as it was exciting.

We hope Leah and J.T.'s story draws you in and doesn't let go until the very last page. We'd love to hear what you think. Write to us at P.O. Box 12271, Toledo, OH 43612 (we'll respond with a signed bookplate, newsletter and bookmark), or visit us on the Web at www.toricarrington.com for hot drawings. And don't miss the other two books in our SLEEPING WITH SECRETS miniseries. Look for *Indecent* in June 2004 and *Wicked* in August.

Here's wishing you love, romance and compelling reading.

Lori & Tony Karayianni
aka Tori Carrington

Books by Tori Carrington

FORBIDDEN

Tori Carrington

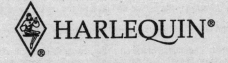

TORONTO • NEW YORK • LONDON
AMSTERDAM • PARIS • SYDNEY • HAMBURG
STOCKHOLM • ATHENS • TOKYO • MILAN • MADRID
PRAGUE • WARSAW • BUDAPEST • AUCKLAND

We warmly dedicate this book to Diana Tidlund aka Moosehog, the coolest biker babe we know! May all your adventures be sweet....

ISBN 0-373-79133-X

FORBIDDEN

www.eHarlequin.com

Printed in U.S.A.

1

EVERY TIME IT RAINED Leah Dubois Burger thought of J. T. West. The way he'd dragged his strong fingers down the flesh of her back, tracing a path to her bottom. He'd branded her, claimed her, all the while vividly reminding her what it meant to be a woman.

Unfortunately, it rained a lot in Toledo, Ohio, in April. And J.T. hadn't been in the city for nearly a year and a half.

And J. T. West was responsible for the biggest mistake of her life.

Leah leaned against the steering wheel of her late model Lexus and stared at the rain pelting the windshield. She'd shut off the car engine so all she heard were the rhythmic drops hitting the hood of the car. Across the parking lot she could make out the blue neon lights of the Kroger store. It was only 7:00 p.m. but the heavy dark clouds had ushered in dusk early making it feel like winter was holding on by its fingernails. A loaf of bread was all she had to buy. She needed it to make Sami lunch in the morning. She pictured her eleven-year-old daughter waiting at their house in Ottawa Hills, finishing the dinner dishes and talking to her father on the phone like she did every night at about this time. Asking when he was going to move back into the house.

Dan…

Leah waited for an emotion, any emotion, to hit her. She'd been married to the man for eleven years and for the past three months they'd been going through post-marriage therapy to try to patch up their marriage. But her ex-husband failed to bruise the outer edges of her thoughts.

J.T.……

The bottom of her stomach dropped out and her heart began pounding harder than the rain against the asphalt. Such a profound reaction, despite that nearly sixteen months had passed since she'd last seen the man. Despite that he had tempted her into an affair that had ended her marriage and plunged her daughter into a preadolescent funk. Yet how could she forget that he'd made her feel alive again for the first time in…well, a very long time. In truth, she hadn't felt so vital, so free, since that one long-ago August when she was sixteen, he barely eighteen, and the summer had seemed to stretch on forever, making it seem like what they had might never end.

But it had ended.

Only to begin again fourteen years later. After she'd married another man. After she'd started a family. After she'd believed she'd long since grown out of her crush on J. T. West.

A passing car's headlights cut a swath through the soggy night, making Leah blink. She reached for the umbrella on the passenger seat, then hesitated, deciding a little cold rain might be just the thing she needed to wash away wayward memories of the few steamy weeks she'd spent loving a man who had twice disappeared from her life as abruptly as he'd appeared.

She walked toward the supermarket even as her brain told her she should run. Within moments her beige blouse was plastered against her skin and her tan slacks were soaked and wet. But she couldn't bring herself to care beyond pushing her thick, blond hair from her face. An uncharacteristic reaction for someone who spent a great deal of time perfecting her conservative yet stylish appearance. First it had been because she was a judge's daughter, then because she was a prominent attorney's wife. But mostly she enjoyed taking care of her appearance because she liked to look good, liked to feel feminine. Which was also why she allowed herself one self-indulgence—the supersexy lingerie she always wore. She caught a glimpse of herself in the automatic glass doors the moment before they opened.

She barely recognized the bedraggled woman staring back at her. The limp, wet hair. The vacant expression. The untidy clothes. She guessed that she should feel something at the sight, but didn't.

She pushed herself forward, blinking at the bright lights. It seemed odd that everyone was going on with life as usual. She didn't know what else she expected. Maybe that they would all pause and look at her as if they knew what she'd been thinking. Or rather whom she'd been thinking about. Whisper comments on her dreadful appearance. Instead the cashiers scanned groceries, the patrons perused the impulse-buy magazines on display at the checkout counter, and the bag boys slid merchandise into white plastic bags, none of them giving her any notice.

All in all, life went on as usual.

Why, then, didn't it feel that way for her?

She absently picked up a shopping basket and cut through an empty line, her steps slow, her mind sluggish. All day she'd been distracted and disoriented. She'd forgotten to wash Sami's basketball jersey and her daughter hadn't been happy about it, Febreze-doused and sporting a spot above the ''U'' in Burger no matter how hard Leah had tried to rub it out. She'd sat through lunch with her sister, Rachel, barely tasting the food and hardly registering her sister's presence beyond how happy she looked now that she and Gabe Wellington had set a date for their wedding. Her father had called while she'd been making meatloaf for dinner and she'd forgotten to add eggs so it had come out dry and cracked. She wasn't sure how she felt that Sami hadn't seemed to notice beyond commenting on how much better her Grandma Burger's meatloaf was, then reaching for the ketchup bottle.

When had life become so…routine? So dull?

"Oh, Leah, if only life was all roses and candlelight," she could hear her mother saying when she'd been stood up the night of her junior prom. "Comfort yourself with the knowledge that when things get bad, it means good times are ahead."

Leah figured she was long overdue for good times. Or even okay times.

Or, at the very least, a few minutes with her mother who had always somehow managed to make her feel better.

But Patricia Dubois had died of breast cancer over a year and a half ago.

Curiously, at the same time Leah had crossed paths with J. T. West again.

She stared down at the can of chicken noodle soup in her hand, not remembering picking it up, and with no real sense of how long she'd been standing staring at it.

"This weather is something else, isn't it?"

Leah looked up at an elderly woman standing nearby. "Isn't it, though?" She managed a feeble smile, put the can in her basket, then moved farther on down the aisle.

Bread. She'd come here for a loaf of bread. She programmed her feet to head in the direction of the bakery section. Maybe a long, hot bath and a book would help ease her out of this strange mood. And chocolate. Lots of chocolate. She stopped at the end of the aisle and rather than continuing toward the bakery section, she backtracked to the racks upon racks of sweets where a nice extra-large bar of Hershey's with almonds was waiting for her.

Along with J. T. West...

She blinked. It wasn't possible. Had to be a trick of her imagination. She'd conjured up his presence through the power of wishful or wistful thinking. But no. The more she blinked, the clearer he became. He was there. Back in Toledo. In the grocery store. Looking at her as if she was the entire reason he was there.

Where she'd been numb, now every nerve ending sparked to glorious, heated life.

Temptation incarnate, J. T. West. Looking better than any one man had a right to.

Standing at the other end of the aisle, leaning a wide shoulder against the shelving, his long, thick jean-clad legs crossed at his booted ankles. His leather jacket remarkably dry, the white T-shirt underneath hugging his abs in all the right places. The only evidence that he'd been out in the rain at all lay in the dampness of his hair. Jet-black hair that swooped down over his forehead, giving his eyes an intense quality even here in the brightly lit supermarket.

It seemed strangely apropos that he'd picked the candy aisle in which to reveal himself. He fit right in among the forbidden sweets. Decadent and illicit.

Oh, God, J. T. West is back.

A shiver ran the length of Leah's body from the top of her head to the very tip of her toes.

She swallowed thickly.

Oh, God, J. T. West is back....

J.T. WASN'T SURE WHY he'd chosen now to reveal his presence to Leah. This moment. He'd rolled back into Toledo on his Harley four days ago. And had been tailing Leah ever since.

Up this close, Leah Dubois Burger looked better than even his memory of her. J.T. shoved his hands deeper into the pockets of his jeans for fear that if he didn't trap them they'd automatically reach out for the woman who looked so hauntingly beautiful—even in the glaring fluorescent lights of the supermarket, even soaked to the bone—it made him ache.

"Hello, Leah."

He stared at the long line of her elegant neck as she slowly swallowed, her gaze fixed on him.

"J.T...."

Something coiled tight in the pit of his stomach at the way his name exited as a hushed breath through her lush, lush lips.

He fought a groan.

How long had he envisioned this moment? When he might come face-to-face with Leah again? Might take in her beautiful features? A month? A year?

No. He knew exactly how long. Since the moment he'd left her sleeping in that ratty motel room exactly sixteen months, three days and fifteen hours ago.

Throughout every waking and sleeping moment since then, she'd been a constant presence in his life. As a memory. A sigh.

And throughout every waking moment he'd cursed that clinging memory. Tried to ban it. Ban her. Make himself forget.

But it was during his dreams when he had no power over the direction of his thoughts that she wiped away all his willpower and held him at her mercy. Until he stood right where he was now. Looking at her. Assessing her. Trying to fathom whether she'd thought about him as much as he had about her.

Somehow he knew that she had thought about him. Thought about them. Could tell by the dilation of the pupils in her dark eyes. The flick of her tongue at the corner of her mouth. The shallowness of her breathing. The tightening of her nipples under her damp blouse that seemed to beg him for attention.

J.T. knew that if he slid his fingers inside the waistband of her slacks he'd find her hot and wet and ready. And right then he wanted that more than anything. More than the food that sustained him. More than the air that he breathed.

More than the risk of his own freedom.

Leah finally broke away and turned toward the shelf. She stuffed a chocolate bar into her basket, began to walk away, then backtracked and put another bar, then another into the basket before she passed him.

J.T. noted that she had yet to say more than his name. As she disappeared at the end of the aisle, he supposed seeing him again after so long was quite a shock for her. She might even be having some trouble convincing herself he was really there.

His mind filled with the ways that he could prove to her that he was back.

2

PLEASE, HURRY.

Leah pushed her few items down the checkout line conveyor belt, mentally praying for the cashier to pick up the pace. She wanted...no, needed to get out of there as quickly as she could. Before J.T....

Someone put a six-pack of Coors on the belt behind her. Her breath froze in her lungs. She didn't have to look to see who it was. She already knew. The brand was J.T.'s.

"Ma'am? Your card, please."

Leah blinked to stare at the cashier. Her card... Her brain distantly registered that she was being asked for her savings card, but she couldn't bring herself to retrieve it from her purse. "No card," she whispered.

The cashier entered a code and began ringing up the purchases.

Leah was acutely aware of J.T.'s presence behind her. Felt a magnetic force drawing her in, affecting the flow of her blood, the direction of her thoughts. Never in her life had she met someone as physically powerful, emotionally mesmerizing as J. T. West. He entered a room and you knew it. If J.T. wanted you, you were loath to refuse him.

The cashier named a price.

Pay…she needed to pay for the groceries.

Leah's brain refused to register the simplest of commands.

She reached into her bag and rummaged around inside for her wallet, her hands trembling wildly. She closed her eyes and took a deep breath…then watched as the contents of her purse dumped out onto the floor at her feet.

She knelt to pick everything up at the same time as J.T.

Leah swallowed thickly. God, he smelled good. Too good. There was something about the way the detergent he used on his clothes combined with the musk of his soap and the rich leather of his jacket that appealed to her on a primal level. Made her think of clear streams and wide-open spaces. And of a passion so wild she forgot who she was.

"Ma'am?" the cashier said again, repeating the price.

In that one moment, Leah forgot not to look up into J.T.'s eyes. Forgot that up this close the intoxicating golden hue would hypnotize her. Tempt her to count the flecks of green in the light brown depths. Lure her into doing things that in her right mind she would never, ever do.

"I've got it." J.T. peeled a couple of bills from a roll he took from the back pocket of his jeans.

"No, really..." Leah stood up, nearly dumping her purse again, only to realize she was too late. J.T. had not only paid for her things, but was now paying for his beer.

She stared at him as he handed her bag to her and gestured toward the door.

Leah knew she should say something. Thank him for buying the groceries. Offer to pay him back. Ask him what he was doing there. But she couldn't seem to bring herself to say anything. Instead she virtually rocketed for her car and climbed in, ignorant of the rain and her appearance.

And unsurprised when J.T. climbed into the passenger's seat next to her.

Her gulp sounded loud in the small confines. She hadn't been prepared for how...intimate the setting would be. With the darkness outside, the rain pelting against the rooftop, the scent of his nearness crowding her senses, it was all she could do not to gasp at the evocativeness of it all.

"When did you get back?"

Leah's words sounded breathy even to her own ears and she wondered if J.T. could hear the *thud-thud* of her heart in the silence of the car.

He squinted at her. "Does it matter?"

No, it didn't. But his response did imply that he'd been back for more than just a day.

The thought made her thighs grow even damper. Knowing that J.T. had been in town for a prolonged period presented her with a whole different viewpoint. Partly because she'd known that when he'd left sixteen months ago, he'd left town completely and she'd figured he'd never come back.

But he had. And for more than a day.

And now he was sitting in her car making her remember with vivid clarity how sweet it was to kiss his skillful mouth. How thrilling it was to have his arms around her.

How very wrong it was for her to want both.

"Dan and I are reconciling," she said.

That got a response from him. He dropped his gaze then squinted through the windshield, headlights from a passing car flickering over his granite features. "You divorced?"

Leah caught her bottom lip between her teeth and also looked away. She nodded, wondering how wise it was to reveal that she was free.

Oh, free was so wrong a word it made her wince. She wasn't any freer now than she had been back then. She and Dan were reconciling. For God's sake, they were even now discussing the date when he might move back into the house. Her daughter,

Sami, talked about her father's return nonstop. Her family had come to accept the reconciliation and plans were being made for a family dinner on Easter, mere weeks away.

And she still wanted the man sitting next to her with a ferocity that scared her to death.

Leah felt J.T.'s hand on her cheek. The thick, callused pad of his thumb felt so natural against her skin that rather than pulling back, she allowed her eyes to drift close and her head to lean into his touch.

"Do you love him?"

Leah felt her chest cave in on her heart. She blinked to look into J.T.'s intense gaze. He'd asked the question of her before. The night they'd first met.

She hadn't answered him then. And she had never asked herself the question again.

"J.T., I don't think this is such a good idea. Sami's waiting for me to get home. I'm glad to see you, happy you're doing well..."

"Kiss me, Leah."

The words were so simple, so straightforward. And had the effect of a bulldozer on all her good intentions.

She crossed the mere inches separating them and did as he requested.

Oh God, oh God, oh God...

He tasted so good. Better than she remembered. Like butterscotch candy and hot, hot man. His lips were soft and malleable. His tongue like a lick of fire as it entered her mouth.

Leah's breath quickened, her blood flowed through her veins enticing her limbs to action. Her fingers found their way to J.T.'s damp hair. Her chest found a way to crush against his across the narrow console. Her mouth slipped and bit and devoured his lips until she was afraid that the fire of his tongue would ignite her entire body.

He caught her chin in his hand and held her steady for long, silent moments, staring into her eyes. "Are you sure this is what you want?" he asked.

Yes.

No!

Leah didn't know what she wanted. She just wanted what she was feeling never to stop.

Her silence appeared all the answer he needed as he hauled her across the console until her bottom rested in his lap and her legs dangled over into the driver's seat. She became instantly aware of his erection, long and hard against her bottom. She moaned and melded her mouth to his, afraid of what might happen if they continued, afraid of what might happen if they didn't. Her fingers found their way to his jacket and pushed open the leather, then shoved up the soft cotton of his T-shirt. She remembered that he was rock-hard everywhere and she quickly discovered that hadn't changed. Except that he seemed to be even more solidly muscular. Leaner. A dangerous energy emanated from him that caught her up in its conflicting current.

She didn't realize he'd opened her blouse until she felt his tongue against the upper swell of her right breast. Leah stretched her neck and gritted her teeth together, shivers traveling down her back then up again, making her tremble from head to foot. J.T. cupped her breast, then squeezed, forcing the flesh upward from the lacy demi cup. He fastened his mouth over her painfully distended nipple and she cried out, digging her fingers deeply into the flesh of his shoulders. She knew a need so powerful it rocked her to the core.

She fumbled for and found his zipper, tugging it down and sliding her fingers inside the cotton of his boxers until she held the very essence of him. His turgid flesh was so long. So thick. So hard. Her mouth watered with the desire to taste him. To coax out his bittersweet semen. To hear him call out her name, his fingers entwined in her hair, tightly holding her to him.

With some awkwardness, she helped him rid her of her slacks and then straddled him, her right knee hitting the console, her left wedged tightly against the door. But she didn't care. All she could concentrate on was how badly she wanted this one man. How hot she was, how hot he was, and how she knew that only he could put out the fire twisting and turning inside her.

She reached to position him against her hungry flesh. She gasped when he grabbed her wrist in a viselike grip.

"No," he ground out.

The air disappeared from Leah's lungs.

"Not like this. Not in a car. Not so soon."

Leah blinked at him, incapable of speech.

J.T. stared at her for a long moment then deposited her back onto the driver's seat. She watched, dumbstruck, as he adjusted his clothing with the same control he did everything else, then he sat back and looked at her, his eyes full of question and mystery.

"It was good seeing you, Leah," he murmured.

Then he climbed out of the car and slammed the door.

J.T. STOOD ALONE in the parking lot, the cool spring rain washing over him as he watched Leah's taillights disappear into the damp night. She had turned toward the big, warm house waiting for her a few miles to the west. The house that over the past twelve years she'd made a home. A place not unlike the hulking house she'd grown up in. He'd visited both places only once and had known instantly that he didn't belong in either. Just as he'd known that Leah hadn't belonged in either his father's rusty trailer or the shabby, no-star motels he'd recently called home.

But if there was one thing he'd come to understand during his thirty-two years—and especially in the past year and a half—it was that outer trappings had very little to do with basic human wants and needs. And if the past thirty minutes were any indication, he wanted...*needed* Leah on a level he couldn't begin to understand. All he knew was that he had to explore what it was. If for no other reason than to tuck her and whatever existed between them neatly into the past, where so far it had refused to rest.

Water dripped down over his face, soaking his T-shirt, running over his jacket, but still he couldn't bring himself to move. What he'd experienced with Leah before had been profound. But what had passed between them a few minutes ago had shaken him to the bone. He hadn't had sex in a car since he was eighteen. And, curiously enough, it had been with Leah. He'd been a hairbreadth away from taking what Leah had just so generously, hungrily offered. Had known such a ferocious desire to bury

himself in her sweet, hot flesh that in that one moment everything else had emerged irrelevant.

Even his freedom.

His gaze cut to a car entering the parking lot from
the opposite direction. A white and blue cruiser em-
blazoned with the words Toledo City Police Department. J.T. shoved his hands deep into the pockets of his jeans, then turned and made his way
toward his bike. He heard the cruiser slowly pass by
him, then continue on as he put on his helmet. He
watched as the officers turned at the end of the lane
then he straddled the wet Harley. He was less than
a mile away from the city line. The cruiser exited
the parking lot onto Secor Road, then disappeared
from site. But the significance of his reaction to it
lingered on, pounding against J.T. much like the
rain.

If he'd needed a reminder of how much he was
putting on the line by coming back to Toledo, by
staying in one place for longer than he knew to be
safe, the innocuous drive-by was it. While the
cruiser and the officers in it hadn't been looking for
him, they might be tomorrow. Or the day after that.
Which didn't leave him much time to accomplish
what he needed to.

The powerful bike started up with a quiet roar,
echoing the emotions pulsing through him. So much
at stake. With no guarantees. But he needed to find

out if she was a bored middle-upper class housewife seeking a bit of fun with a bad boy from her younger days. Or if Leah Dubois Burger loved him. And he wasn't leaving until he found out.

3

"I NEED THAT PERMISSION SLIP for the class trip today. And I can't find my blue volleyball shorts."

Leah squinted against the early-morning sun slanting in through the French doors as she stacked thinly sliced pieces of turkey breast onto a whole-wheat slice of bread. Bread that she had picked up at the market the night before last. Bread that had been the cause of long, restless nights filled with yearnings for a man she shouldn't be yearning for.

"You can't find your volleyball shorts because they're in the laundry room waiting to be washed." She tore lettuce apart and added it to the sandwich. "And what class trip?"

"You didn't wash my shorts?"

Sami finally stepped out of the glare of the light. It never ceased to amaze Leah that an eleven-year-old girl could have so much to be angry about. Her daughter's blue eyes flashed and her light brown hair seemed to crackle with electricity.

"No," Leah said carefully, cutting the sandwich into two even halves then putting it into a baggie.

"I didn't wash your shorts, Sam. And you didn't answer me about the trip."

Her daughter continued to ignore her question, turning on her heel and stalking to the laundry room just off the dining area. Leah put the sandwich into a backpack along with a pear, carrot sticks and a juice pack and watched Sami pick through the laundry basket for her shorts. The navy blue material was wrinkled but otherwise unsoiled.

"I can't possibly wear these!" Sami cried.

Leah stretched her neck, looked at her watch and asked again, "What class trip?"

Sami glared at her, stalked back across the kitchen to the crowded desk built into the cabinets, then fished out a slip of paper in among the bills. "This one."

Sami slapped the paper onto the counter into a dollop of mustard then stalked from the room. Leah read the slip as she wiped the mustard from the back of it. It seemed two weeks ago her daughter's History teacher had requested permission for Sami to go on a class trip to the Toledo Museum of Art. Leah was pretty certain she didn't remember her daughter saying anything about the trip. And she'd gone through the bills stacked on her desk two nights ago and hadn't seen the slip. But considering her own state of mind as of late, she couldn't bring herself to lay the blame completely on her daughter.

To say she hadn't been on top of things recently would be akin to saying coffee was black.

Speaking of coffee…

She stared longingly at the empty carafe on the counter behind her, then winced at the sound of her daughter's bedroom door slamming.

Leah briefly closed her eyes, trying to remember that it wasn't all that long ago that she and Sami had been best friends. Well, okay, not best friends. But there had been a level of respect and trust and warmth there that Leah had once shared with her own mother.

Now it seemed she could do nothing right in the eleven-year-old's eyes. If she breathed, she was doing it wrong. And on some days she found herself teetering between wanting to lock the girl in the basement or run away entirely.

Of course, she'd known the exact moment when the tides had turned. The night nearly a year and a half ago when she had sat Sami down and told her that she and her father were separating.

And the reason for their separation had been the very man who was causing her distraction now.

Two days had passed since she'd run into J. T. West at the market. Two days since he'd climbed into her car and she'd remembered all at once what it was be like to just…be. To feel like a woman. Not somebody's mother. Not somebody's daughter.

Not somebody's ex working toward reconciliation. Then she'd practically mauled him in the front seat.

It had been two days since she'd heard from him and was left to wonder if he was still in town. Two days since she'd told herself that nothing had really happened between them. They'd merely kissed. Nothing more. Nothing less. And there was nothing wrong in that because, technically, she and Dan weren't reconciled yet. They were still divorced. He didn't live in the house.

And her arguments weren't making a dent in the enormous guilt that coated her insides like thick, black tar.

Leah squeezed her eyes shut. Worse than the guilt, though, were thoughts of J.T. that could be called nothing but carnal. And burned in her mind was the memory of his face when she first caught sight of him in that supermarket. At that moment it had seemed like barely a day had passed since she'd last seen him, rather than sixteen long, brutal months. Months when she'd tried to pick up the pieces of her broken heart and her broken life and glue them back together, even though she was convinced there wasn't enough superglue in the world to handle the monumental job.

She slowly licked her lips, remembering that when she'd kissed J.T.'s mouth her desire had skyrocketed, dampened not at all by the time that had passed, by everything that had happened between then and now. If anything, she wanted him even worse now than ever.

And for two full nights she had twisted and turned in bed, wanting him with an intensity that left her breathless.

"I'm borrowing your blue sweatpants for the game."

Leah blinked Sami's angry face into focus. Her daughter narrowed her eyes at her as she shook the pants in question. The jersey pants were part of a lounge set, not true sweatpants, but she wasn't up to arguing the point that Sami had at least two pair of acceptable shorts tucked away somewhere in her own dresser drawers.

Leah signed the permission slip then put it in the front zipper of the backpack. She handed the pack to her daughter. "Fine."

"You're not driving me to school this morning?"

The day was warm and sunny. The elementary school Sami attended wasn't a third of a mile away. Yet she normally did drive her daughter.

She turned and gathered her own lunch, which consisted of a tuna salad. "No, I'm going in the opposite direction. I have an early class."

Sami sighed and rolled her eyes. "I don't know why you have to go to school. School is for kids. And you're not a kid."

Like she needed to be told that.

But shortly after Dan had left, while she'd still been trying to figure out her affair with J.T., she'd decided she wanted to go back and finish the business degree she'd given up when she'd married Dan and had Sami.

"Maybe you'll understand when you're older," she said. "You'd better get going or you'll be late."

"I can't wait until Dad comes back so this house can get back to normal," Sami mumbled, then grabbed her sweater from the coatrack near the front door and slammed out of the house.

Leah stared after her, suppressing a full body shudder. Normal? She wanted to ask her daughter what exactly constituted normal. Leah living her life strictly for her husband and child? Making sure jerseys and shorts were clean, appointments kept, the gas tank full so she could run errands to pick up their things, do their errands, take them to school and to work?

It appeared she and Sami were overdue for another talk. Not that she thought it would make a difference. Leah had the sinking sensation that her daughter and she would never see eye to eye again.

She grabbed her own jacket and shrugged into it while holding her books and lunch and juggling the keys to lock the door after herself. The Lexus SUV sat in the driveway instead of the garage because

Sami had decided to paint her bike and the still-wet bike in question was sitting where Leah's car usually sat.

She opened the back door of the car and dropped her lunch and books onto the seat, then she slid into the driver's seat. She started the car, her gaze drawn to the passenger seat where J.T. had sat two nights before. But he wasn't sitting there now. Instead a small white bag bearing the logo of a nearby bakery along with an extra-large cup of coffee and a single peach-colored rose sat in the middle of the seat.

Leah's heart turned over in her chest as she breathed in the aroma of fresh pastry and coffee filling the car. The sound of a motorcycle motor pulled her attention to the street behind her. Was J.T. there? Was he watching to see her reaction to finding his little surprise? She didn't see anything but the regular morning activity of neighbors leaving for work, kids walking to school, the newsboy delivering newspapers.

She knew a moment of anticipation so overwhelming her thighs trembled.

J.T. was still in town....

And the prospect of seeing him made her hot all over…and more than a little scared.

J.T. SAT PARKED UNDER A TREE and behind a mini-van a half block up and watched Leah scan the street, undoubtedly looking for him. He knew from having gotten some idea of her routine the past week that she had an early class this morning. And after watching her light go on and off every half hour between eleven and one before he'd headed home last night, he suspected she needed a jolt of caffeine this morning. Seeing her daughter storm from the house, glare at the closed door then stalk off, told him his efforts were likely doubly appreciated.

J.T.'s fingers tightened on the handgrips of the old bike. Of course the surprise had been more than a thoughtful gesture. In truth, he'd wanted Leah to know that he was still there, and that he wasn't going anywhere anytime soon.

Since kissing her again after so long, and discovering that the explosive attraction that had originally drawn them together was still there, he realized that his mission might take more time than he'd thought. It was going to be a challenge to dig deep beyond that molten attraction and see if something more substantial, more significant, more binding existed. And time was what he intended to give himself. Despite the deep craving that burrowed inside him every time he thought of her, saw her, what he needed transcended the physical.

They'd gone that route before. And it had left them both standing right where they were now. Leah divorced and considering reconciling with her ex-husband. Him wanting her so badly he had night sweats. And both of them wondering *what if*.

Basically it left them nowhere.

Leah backed out of the driveway of her mammoth brick colonial-style house and drove in the other direction. An older man wearing a wool housecoat opened the door to the house in front of him, bent to pick up his morning paper, then stared at J.T. with open curiosity and suspicion.

J.T. gave him a small nod, started up his bike, then turned around and went in the opposite direction from where Leah had gone, the morning air brisk against his skin, the sun making him squint.

Not ready. Completely in the dark. Ill-prepared. All three descriptions fit where he stood right now. When it came to relationships, his experience was between zero and nil simply because never in his life had he had the chance to learn the art. Lord knew his father, Delbert, had done all he could. As the son of a mechanic, Delbert had grown up without much use for a dictionary and more than a handful of words. And he'd raised his own son the same way, making J.T. forever the outsider when they traveled from town to town in search of a better job, a better life. To J.T.'s way of thinking, the only time they had achieved that goal was during that brief stretch the summer of his eighteenth year when he'd met fiery, sixteen-year-old Leah and had been given his first taste of the woman who would haunt him from then on.

J.T.'s mind circled back to his father. Del hadn't said one way or another whether he approved of J.T.'s decision to go on to college when he was offered a scholarship, but J.T. had suspected he'd been disappointed his son hadn't followed in his footsteps and became a mechanic. And the old man had merely nodded when that road had became a dead end two years later, leaving a young woman dead, sending a falsely accused J.T. on the run and destroying any future he might have imagined for himself.

Over the course of the next ten years he'd ridden from place to place, never staying anywhere for more than a few weeks at a time, a way of life his father's own traveling had well prepared him for. In the beginning he'd worked various minimum-wage jobs to cover his expenses, but that required lying about his social security number, his name. Then he'd rented a room from an old man, not unlike his father, who had taught him carpentry. And he'd found the perfect job for a man who couldn't afford to stick around long. A free agent, he was paid a flat fee, erasing any need for uncomfortable questions about his past and his identity.

He smoothly shifted gears, resisting the urge to increase his speed when traffic opened up. Considering his resistance to ending up a mechanic, he was surprised to find he liked working with his hands. More than that, he enjoyed the feel of a virgin piece of wood under his fingers, watching as it slowly told him how to cut it, then gave in to his will and became furniture that was not only functional but bore the mark of its original beauty.

Not all that unlike the way Leah opened up under his hands, freeing the girl he once knew as spunky and smart and gutsy, afraid of nothing. Passionate, greedy, demanding. So unlike the Leah of today whose eyes were devoid of any emotion at all and whose movements seemed automated, uninspired.

She had once told him that she loved the feel of his rough skin against hers....

J.T. set his jaw. Of all the women he'd been with in his life, including the one that had ended up stealing his freedom, he had yet to determine what it was about Leah Dubois Burger that touched him so profoundly.

But if there was one thing he planned to do before leaving Toledo, Ohio, it was not only to unearth if she felt the same way about him, but whether or not she could accept who he had become.

4

"MEET ME AT TEN TONIGHT."

Leah stood outside her car in the University of Toledo parking lot later that day, the midday sun warm against her face, her fingers trembling as they held the small piece of paper that had been under her windshield wiper. The longing that had been burning through her veins for the past week sent a warm shiver careening through her body. J.T. had written the name of a small bar and where it was just outside the western city line. He hadn't signed his name. But she didn't think any of the twenty-year-olds in her classes had left her the note. No, it was definitely J.T.

She stuffed the paper into the pocket of her slacks then unlocked the door to her car and climbed in, sitting for long moments staring through the window.

She swallowed hard, the sound loud in the confines of the closed car. She couldn't go. Wouldn't.

Her watch chimed off the hour and she absently glanced at it. It took her a moment to register that she was due to meet Dan at the therapist's office in half an hour, the one time a month when they met at lunchtime as opposed to after five.

She picked up her cell phone, lightly rolling her thumbs over the numbers. She'd never cancelled a session before. But how could she possibly go and face her ex-husband and the counselor feeling the way she did?

And how did she feel?

Flustered. Needy. Alive. Like the woman she'd once been who hadn't expressed her sexiness through lingerie hidden under her clothes, but in everything she did.

Stupid.

She blinked at the last word, her movements even more sluggish than they'd been recently. Hadn't she gone this route before? Hadn't she put everything on the line for a man who had a history of disappearing? Who offered her nothing beyond the moment, only the here and now? Hadn't she sacrificed her marriage, her relationship with her daughter and the only way of life she had known for a few hours of escape in another man's arms?

She reached to slip the cell phone back into her purse and it vibrated. She looked at the display. Her sister, Rachel.

Leah idly considered not answering.

Rachel was a year younger and a whole world

happier than she was. In two months she'd be marrying the man of her dreams. A man with a past even darker than Leah's was, but a heart as big as Ohio. All you had to do was look at Gabe Wellington to see how much he loved Rachel.

Had Dan ever looked at her that way? She briefly closed her eyes, trying to remember. No, he hadn't. Maybe. Way back in the beginning.

"For a minute there I thought you weren't going to pick up," her sister said when Leah finally answered just before the call would have rerouted to voice mail.

I wish I hadn't. "Class ran over." Liar.

"What are you doing for lunch?"

She glanced at her watch again though she didn't have to. She knew what time it was every moment of every day, if only because it seemed to drag by. "I have to be at the counselor's in twenty minutes."

"Oh."

Leah caught the flat tone of her sister's voice as she said the simple word. "And that would mean what, exactly?"

A pause then, "You don't sound like yourself. What's going on?"

Rachel. The smarter of the two sisters who had not only made it through college, but had gone on to law school to become an attorney and a city councilwoman.

Sometimes Leah hated her.

But she'd always love her.

"Nothing. I guess I just didn't sleep well last night. And Sami read me the riot act this morning for not washing her volleyball shorts."

"And you're going to counseling like that? Maybe you should cancel and meet me for a margarita."

Leah sighed and relaxed slightly into the driver's seat, wondering if the muddled emotions crowding her chest would ever leave. "I can't tell you how good that sounds."

"So do it then. And meet me at Carmel's in ten."

Leah opened her mouth to refuse but Rachel had already hung up.

She absently pushed disconnect and stared at the cell for a long moment. She'd never canceled a session before. Surely this one time couldn't do any harm.

She called Dan's office first only to learn he'd already left.

Maybe she should go. Dan was probably already on his way, if he wasn't already there. Either way, he would have his cell switched off.

She dialed the therapist's office next and told the assistant she couldn't make it but that she'd be there for their regularly scheduled meeting.

She disconnected, put the cell back in her bag,

then pulled it back out again to switch the receiver off, routing all incoming calls directly to voice mail. The instant she did it, she felt ten pounds lighter, though it did nothing to stop the moths fluttering around in her belly.

Oh, boy, did she ever need this margarita.

"GABE WANTS ME TO MOVE into his place after the wedding," Rachel told her from where she sat across from her at Carmel's Mexican Restaurant.

Leah fingered the coarse salt lining on her extra-large margarita glass then licked her finger. She'd never been much of a drinker and knew from experience that she wouldn't be able to drink more than a quarter of the concoction before her, but somehow it made her feel better to sip from a mammoth glass than a smaller one.

"And the problem is?"

"The problem is I just bought my own house, had it completely renovated and just moved into it three months ago. I don't want to move again." She sipped at her own margarita then crossed her arms on top of the table. "Besides, the thought of living in the mausoleum he calls home gives me the creeps."

Leah cracked a halfhearted smile. "It can't be that bad. The Wellington place is a part of Toledo history."

"Then Gabe should turn it into a museum or something."

Leah didn't know much about the Wellington estate beyond the sweeping grounds and the towering castlelike spires. She'd fished for an invitation from her sister once or twice, but it sounded like Rachel spent as little time at the house as possible and was trying to find ways to get out of going to the dark manor instead of inventing reasons to have to be there. "It's not all that much bigger than where we grew up."

"Yes, but our house is different. Even when it was just Dad and us there, it still seemed…I don't know, like home."

Leah cocked her head to the side and considered her pretty sister. "Don't you think that's how Gabe feels about his house? Especially since he doesn't have any family left?"

Rachel ran her fingers through her short, spiky brown hair and made a face. "God, I knew I'd live to regret you seeing a therapist. You're even starting to sound like one. The next thing you know you'll be diagnosing my condition and prescribing me Xanax or something."

Rachel glowered at her, making Leah glad that she could forget about her own problems for a precious stretch of time and focus instead on her sister's. Why was it so much easier to fix other people's problems than your own? Maybe because the emotion factor didn't figure into the equation. Maybe because as an outsider your opinion was a little more objective.

Maybe because you knew that your own problems were easily solved and you were purposely ignoring them for that very reason.

Rachel narrowed her eyes at her. "Uh-oh. I know that look. What's going on?"

Leah blinked. She'd forgotten that Rachel had been the first one to pick up on her affair with J.T. nearly a year and a half ago. And here she was having an escapist drink with the only person who could finger what was going on.

"Actually," Rachel continued, "now that I think about it, you've been acting strangely for a few days now."

Leah cleared her throat. "I have not been acting strangely."

"Yes, you have. It's been taking you forever to answer the phone. Usually you pick up on the first or second ring. And even when I do get you, you sound distracted and absentminded."

Leah shrugged, her gaze darting around the restaurant before returning to settle on her sister. "Maybe there is something going on. And maybe there isn't. I don't know. I haven't quite figured it out yet myself." She stared at her drink. "Would it be all right to say that I'm really not up to talking about it right now?''

"Is it Dan?''

Leah wished she were anywhere but there in that one moment.

No, scratch that. Despite everything, she wouldn't want to be anywhere else. If she were back at the house, she'd be climbing the walls until Sami came home from her volleyball game after school. If she had gone to the counseling session, she'd be sitting next to Dan trying to work out a situation her mind wasn't completely on right now. And if she was with J.T....

Well, he wasn't much of an option, was he? Even though his gift of a coffee, a roll and a rose that morning and his note this afternoon told her he was nearby, she didn't know how to get in touch with him. Not that she would. It was just that knowing being with him wasn't an option helped.

Marginally.

She shifted in her seat. "I really don't want to talk about it right now.''

Rachel was silent for a few moments as she studied her, then her gaze cut to the approaching waitress.

"Saved by the food,'' her sister said, offering up a smile.

Leah smiled back at her and moved her glass so her salad could be put down in front of her.

Within moments they were alone again. Leah speared the crisp lettuce with forced enthusiasm while Rachel did the same across from her.

"I know I can be a little pushy sometimes," Rachel said quietly.

Leah raised her brows in feigned shock.

"Cut it out." Rachel chewed a bite then swallowed. "I suppose what I'm trying to say is that, well, you know I'm here whenever you're ready to talk, don't you?" she said quietly, her hazel eyes steady.

Yes, she did know that. And that simple knowledge calmed the edginess in her, however slightly. But how could she talk about what she had yet to understand?

Leah nodded, feeling ridiculously close to tears. "I know. Thanks."

IT WAS NEARLY TEN-THIRTY and there was no sign of Leah.

J.T. sat at the end of the long bar, his fingers wrapped around a still-full beer bottle that was growing warmer by the minute. In the corner the jukebox played an old Johnny Cash song while at the two pool tables four men traded shots, the winners destined to play the owners of the next quarters on the nicked lips of the tables. J.T. had seen his share of drinking holes and this one was better than most, but not as good as some he'd been in.

He'd long ago discovered that a different set of rules existed in bars. No matter who you were, where you came from or whom you were there to meet, it was your business, as long as you didn't start any problems for others and paid your tab. And if you said just enough to make you friendly, but not too much to make others curious, your face was forgotten as soon as the other men turned their backs, making you just another guy looking to knock back a few brews after work.

J.T.'s gaze slid back toward the door as another just such guy walked in.

He stared down at his beer.

He'd been aware of the odds of Leah's not showing. But he had still hoped she would come. He needed to talk to her. And the only way to do that was in public. Because when they were in private... well, suffice it to say he had a hard time keeping his hands to himself and they didn't get much talking done. As for this particular bar as his choice of public places, well, he'd wanted to make anonymity attractive to her. If he'd chosen a restaurant or someplace closer to her home then the risk of her running into someone she knew would have been high.

But he admitted that perhaps he had jumped the gun a bit when it came to timing. He should have waited a little longer before suggesting they meet.

The only problem was he couldn't wait. The more time that passed, the more he wanted to have Leah. In his bed. Writhing under his body. Her thighs spread wide for him as her back arched up to meet him. Every second that he wasn't able to do that ticked by like an eternity until the next second and the next eternity. He felt like he could have died and been reborn at least ten times since he'd rolled back into town. He threw himself into his work refurbishing the old Victorian farmhouse a few miles from the bar, but had to pace himself lest he work himself right out of a reason to stay in the house.

The door opened.

Another faceless man entered.

J.T. picked up the beer bottle and swallowed deeply from it, barely registering that it was warm and tasted like deer piss. He put it back down, fished a couple of bills from his pocket then stepped toward the jukebox. It looked like his only options were to go back to the empty farmhouse or stick around here and get stinking drunk.

LEAH WRAPPED TREMBLING fingers around the doorknob to the Lantern's Light Tavern and slowly pulled, entering the bar before she could change her mind again. She'd approached the bar no fewer than five times only to head back to her car parked around back. At one point she'd even driven halfway home before hanging a U-turn and coming back to the bar....

Coming back to J.T.

She'd spotted his bike right out front so she knew he was still there. Although she couldn't really figure out why. Dan would never have waited more than fifteen minutes for her before leaving. She shivered at the change in temperature and temperament, wondering how long J.T. would have waited. Another fifteen minutes? A half hour? An hour?

All night?

She still had on her slacks and blouse that she'd worn that morning. She hadn't wanted to make a fuss for fear that Sami would pick up on what was going on. As it turned out her daughter had been too wrapped up in her own drama, something to do with her best friend siding with another girl during the volleyball game. Much telephoning between the three girls ensued. When she'd left, Sami seemed to have patched everything up with her best friend, Courtney, and she'd been sprawled across her bed talking about a new boy at school. She'd barely given her mother a halfhearted wave when Leah had told her she was going to Aunt Rachel's to help her sort through some stuff for the wedding.

And now here she stood, in the middle of a dimly lit bar, her ears filled with the sound of glass clinking, beer being poured and pool sticks hitting cue balls, looking for a man who compelled her to do things she knew she shouldn't. Looking for J.T.

The sound of a few guitar strums floated on the alcohol-infused air. She looked in the direction of the jukebox and found J.T. bending over it, his back to her.

Her heart lodged tightly in her throat.

J. T. West filled out a pair of jeans like no man she had ever known could. The worn, faded denim was slightly loose around his slender waist and fit him snuggly around his hindquarters, making her fingers itch with the desire to run them down the soft cotton, probing the steel-hard flesh beneath.

He slowly turned, as if sensing her presence, her stare. Leah felt frozen to the spot as her gaze flicked up the denim of his shirt, catching sight of the tanned, hard chest at the neck before staring directly into his simmering golden brown eyes.

In that one moment everything but this moment ceased to exist for her. The bar. The worries of her class. The complaints of her sister. The concerns of her daughter. All she could hear was the thump of the bass in the song and her own heartbeat. Her palms and other, more intimate, parts of her body grew wet, her breasts tightened and her lips longed for the feel of J.T.'s mouth on hers.

Neither of them moved for long, long moments. Then, finally, J.T. pushed from the old-fashioned, upright jukebox and crossed to hold his hand out to her.

Leah gazed at his large, callused fingers and the dark hair kissing his forearms, then blinked back into his eyes.

"Dance with me?"

Leah's hand shook so violently she was sure J.T. could see it as she slowly placed it in his. A hot, hot shiver rode through her body as she wondered why she felt that accepting his invitation meant so much more than just a dance....

5

LEAH SMELLED OF THE SUBTLE SCENT of gardenias and one-hundred-percent sweet, hot female.

J.T. slowly tugged her until she stood mere millimeters away. The very tips of her breasts brushed against his chest. The insistent throbbing of his manhood pulsed almost painfully, full with desire for this woman who'd haunted him throughout so much of his life. He rested his right hand on her hip, fighting the urge to press her to him until nothing separated them but their clothing.

It had been so long. Too long. But to give in to his craving to claim her now would only take them where they had already gone. And he wanted more, so much more.

"You waited," she said quietly next to his ear.

He tightened his grip on her hand and led her in the slow dance, using every ounce of self-restraint he had to keep from rushing things. "I waited."

He caught the scent of something evocatively familiar. The smell of lemons. And immediately he was transported to the first time they'd ever danced, fourteen years ago on one steamy summer's eve. The entire campsite had gathered for dinner at the pavilion and the park owners had brought in a country band to entertain those who wanted to make a night of it. By midnight most of the campers had gone back to their trailers or tents, leaving just a few behind.

He and Leah had been two of them.

And she'd asked him to dance.

J.T. closed his eyes now, breathing in the lemony scent of her hair. He found it incredible that she still used the same shampoo that she had way back then. Found it incredible that the mouthy, straightforward, gutsy teenager she had been had turned into the hesitant, self-doubting, fearful woman he now held.

She took her hand briefly from his and wiped her palm on her slacks then returned it to his grip, her smile wavering before she turned her head in the other direction.

What had happened during their years apart to make her change? Or had she changed at all? Was his memory painting a picture of her that he wanted to see but that had no basis in reality? Was this Leah the real one?

No. He had only to think of their brief, unexpected, white-hot affair a year and a half ago to know that the Leah he danced with now was not the woman he'd once known. He knew that because for a brief, exciting time she had turned back into that young woman who had the world and everything in it at her beautiful feet. The judge's daughter whose only care in the world was how to satisfy her own curious appetites. And J.T. had been the first man she'd welcomed between her toned thighs.

"Josh, I…"

Every muscle in J.T.'s body tightened.

It seemed forever since anyone had used his given name. And since warning Leah against it the last time they'd met, she hadn't used it, either. No, he hadn't told her the reason he went by his initials now instead of the name he'd been called his entire life. She'd merely accepted that it was something he couldn't share.

That she was using the name now told him he wasn't going to like what he was going to hear.

"Shhh," he said, drawing her closer.

He heard her breath catch and felt her breasts heave slightly against his chest. He suppressed a groan. Did the woman have even the slightest idea how she affected him? Did she know that right now he wanted her so badly he was nearly bursting with his need for her? Did she know that not a day went by that he didn't think about her, remember how it had been between them and hunger after her with an intensity that left him powerless to concentrate on anything but the memory of her?

He put his boot between her shoes and nudged her legs apart, naturally filling the gap with his thigh. She gave a small gasp as his taut muscles rested against her swollen womanhood. Oh, yeah, he knew she wanted him. She always had. It was the one weakness he could use against her.

The problem lay in that he didn't want to use anything against her. Especially not her own betraying emotions.

"I was just remembering the first time we ever danced," he whispered in her ear, teasing the delicate shell with his breath and watching a shiver wash down the delicate cord of her neck, coaxing tiny bumps over her arms. Her neatly trimmed blonde hair seemed to tremble with the reaction he was inciting in her. "Do you remember, Leah?"

She didn't indicate one way or another if she'd heard.

J.T. stared at a spot beyond her, allowing the images of that long ago summer to take over. "I remember the heaviness of the air right before it rained later that night. I remember the sounds of the singer's voice and the chirp of the crickets. The smell of straw and your hair." He pressed his chin against the side of her head. "The way you looked up at me, so hungry, so confident."

Leah went briefly still in his arms.

J.T. tightened his grip on her. "And I thought to

myself, 'This is a woman who knows what she wants. And I'm going to give it to her.'"

"I wasn't a woman, I was a girl."

J.T. pulled back slightly. "No, Leah. You were a woman." He grinned. "I'm convinced that you've been one since the day you were born."

The song drew to an end and Leah attempted to pull away. J.T. didn't allow her the escape. The advantage of his having fed so much money into the jukebox was that he knew which songs would play next.

He brushed his cheek against her hair. "Then you kissed me," he said quietly.

She dropped her gaze to stare at the front of his shirt, then seemed unsatisfied with that and looked restlessly around the bar. "*You* kissed me, if I remember correctly," she said so quietly he nearly didn't hear her.

He shook his head as the next song finally clicked on. "No, Leah. You kissed me." He pressed his lips against her temple, resisting the urge to re-create the moment. But in order to re-create it, she would have to make the first move. Just like she had back then. "You kissed me as if you couldn't help yourself."

"That…that was a long time ago."

J.T. pulled back enough to stare down into her eyes. "Was it? Because right now I'm feeling like it was five minutes ago."

He watched as her pupils dilated in her dark eyes. Oh, yes, he could tell she was feeling the same way. Yearning for that carefree moment when they'd first explored their burning attraction for each other. But his telling and her admitting were two completely different things. And he knew she wasn't anywhere near confessing how she felt. And he also suspected he knew the reason why. Hell, he spent half his time asking himself what it was that he felt for her. And the other half wanting her so badly he throbbed with the power of the need.

She licked her lips. J.T. visually inhaled the movement, knowing it was the prelude to a kiss.

But rather than leaning toward him, she pulled away. "I…I shouldn't be here. I've really got to go."

J.T. resisted the urge to hold her still, to prevent her from leaving. Instead he released his hold on her and watched as she clutched her purse closer to her side and moved toward the door.

He was losing her and he didn't know how to stop it.

LEAH KNEW A DESPERATION to escape so intense her knees shook. It wasn't fair that J.T. had come back. It wasn't fair that he was reminding her of times better off forgotten. It wasn't fair that he made her want him so fully that she felt she'd die if she didn't kiss him, feel him, make love to him...*now*.

She moved toward the door to the bar as quickly as she could, short of running. She shouldn't have come here. It had been foolish to think she could tell J.T. that she couldn't see him again. Look into his eyes and utter the words, "It's over. I've moved on with my life and it's time for you to do the same."

Instead she hadn't hesitated to step into his arms for a dance, her hand in his, their bodies slowly swaying seeming the most natural thing in the world.

"We fit."

She remembered J.T. whispering words to that effect on the very night he'd reminded her of. He hadn't been saying the words to her. Rather it had seemed he'd been talking to himself, his voice so full of wonder and conviction that they'd reverberated through her, changing her life forever.

She pushed the door open and took deep gulps of the chilly spring night air as if she'd just run a marathon. *Changing her life forever*. What a childish, stupid thing to think. Fine for a sixteen-year-old experiencing her first real brush with puppy love. Ridiculous for a woman of thirty with an eleven-year-old daughter.

She wondered what Dr. McKenna would say if

she told him. Would he tell her that her reactions to J.T. were some sort of pre-middle-aged grab at what used to be? A return to the past, to less troubled times? A time when she didn't have adult responsibilities and all that went along with them?

"Leah."

Her step faltered at the sound of her name on J.T.'s lips. He'd followed her. Somewhere deep inside she'd known he would. And somewhere near that knowledge was also the relief, and the grief, that he had.

She swiveled toward him, the air and distance between them allowing her a measure of sanity. "I can't see you again, J.T."

He squinted at her in the near darkness, his face stern as if carved from granite. "You're not seeing me now."

Leah's throat felt so tight she was surprised her breathing didn't sound like panting. "I've seen you twice in the past three days."

"I need to talk to you."

She shook her head adamantly. "That's what I told myself. That's the reason why I came here. To talk. But we don't talk, J.T. We never talk. Whenever we're within touching distance both of us seem to lose the ability to speak."

"We're talking now."

She laughed humorlessly and backed a short ways

away, feeling an almost magnetic pull toward him and fighting it for all she was worth. "It doesn't count. We're just talking about talking." She shook her head and clutched her purse to her stomach as if the action could keep her from moving toward him.

"I've moved on with my life, J.T.," she said, somehow finding the words she'd rehearsed all afternoon, then during the drive out. "I'm back in school. I'm going to counseling with my ex-husband in the hopes of reconciling. And my daughter...well, my daughter needs me to be there for her."

He was silent for a long moment, making her wonder if she'd said the words at all. And if she had, if he could understand what they meant.

"And you?" he asked quietly. "What do you need, Leah?"

No fair. It wasn't fair for him to ask her that question.

He slowly held up his hand up. "What do you want?"

She turned toward her car parked around the back of the lot, out of view of passing traffic. She hadn't done it on purpose, but it seemed that everything connected to J.T. was done in secret. Was bad. Forbidden.

"I want you to leave me alone," she whispered.

But she hadn't said it loud enough for him to hear.

Rather the words had been for her ears only, as if some frightened part of her believed that by saying them she could make them so.

She rounded the building, nearly ran into a Dumpster, then rounded it, getting her keys from her purse.

"I didn't quite make out your last words."

Leah didn't realize that J.T. had grasped her arm and turned her to face him until she was staring up into his too handsome, too rugged face.

"I said that I want you to leave me alone."

Her heart crashed against her rib cage, the sound of her own words like a knife to her chest.

"Do you?" he asked. "Because if you do, I'll leave town right now. Tonight."

Leah felt like she'd never take an unlabored breath again. Standing there looking into a face made familiar by all the times she'd seen it in her dreams, nurtured it in her mind, she wanted the exact opposite of what she was saying.

She licked her lips several times. "Yes. That's what I want." The words grew quieter with each she said until the last one was nearly silent.

They stood like that for long moments, neither of them saying anything, both of them staring at each other, only the sound of passing cars on the other side of the building and the exhaust fan from the back kitchen breaking the utter silence of the night.

Then J.T. released her arm and stepped back.

Panic ballooned in Leah's stomach and she nearly cried out. His movements had been slow but it seemed like he'd just cast her aside like so much garbage.

"Please," she said, stepping toward him. "You've got to understand…"

"Understand what, Leah?" he asked. "I see no room for misunderstanding in your words."

"But I need you to understand my motivations for saying them."

"You told me why. You've moved on with your life."

Her throat threatened to close. Had she really moved on? Or was she treading the same waters she'd swum through before, trying to find the stream that eluded her?

"Why?" she whispered.

She'd promised herself she wouldn't ask him that question. Wouldn't probe into the reasons for his return. But ultimately she couldn't help herself. She needed to know why he'd come back. Why he was in Toledo. And why he appeared to want to talk to her so badly.

"Why did you come back?"

"For the same reason you came here tonight, Leah. I needed to see you again."

His words struck a chord deep within her.

"I needed to convince myself that my mind wasn't playing tricks on me. That I do want you the way I always have."

Leah's knees wavered beneath her and she clutched her purse as though it could help support her.

"I needed to see if the earth still shakes when you kiss me."

The sound of the traffic and fan disappeared, leaving nothing but the thud-thud of her heart. Slowly her grip on her purse loosened until the small clutch dropped to the ground and she was stepping over it to see if J. T. West was still capable of making the earth shake for her, too.

She stood close enough to kiss him, their noses almost touching, her fingers probing the line of his jaw, the slope of his cheek, the ridge of his brow. She stared into his eyes, smelling beer on his breath, the musk of his skin, feeling his heat as if it were her own. She leaned her head to the right, then moved it to the left, then slowly pressed her lips against his. His skin was dry and hot. His perpetual stubble prickled her chin.

Before she knew that was what she was going to do, she was sighing into him, her body automatically molding against his as if unable to hold itself upright anymore without his aid. She flicked her tongue out and moistened his top lip then slid it into his mouth, coaxing him to open for her.

His eyes were dark and unreadable as he watched her and she watched him back. *Kiss me,* she wanted to say. *Kiss me now like you used to back then.*

And then he was.

Leah heard a plaintive whimper and realized it had come from her own throat.

She tilted her head back as J.T. ran his fingertips along the length of her jaw, then rubbed his thumb over her cheek, turning her face so he could meet her mouth more fully. His tongue slowly swept around her mouth and along the ridges of her teeth before he withdrew it and sucked her bottom lip between his.

Leah was suddenly boneless, her muscles melting to liquid. Nothing existed beyond this moment, beyond this kiss, beyond J.T. and the cravings of their bodies. She moved closer to him until her pelvis met his, her breasts crushed against the wall of his chest. She curved her arms around his waist and tried to pull him even closer, though the laws of nature prevented it. Her breathing grew ragged, her womanhood pulsed, the dampness between her legs growing along with her desire to have J.T. here, now.

He must have been on the same page because he swiveled her until her bottom rested against the back of a wooden storage locker. Then he was boosting her up, his fingers on her knees prying her legs apart. He stepped into the space he'd made, his hard manhood pressing insistently against her needy femininity. He slid the top buttons of her blouse open, then slipped his hand inside, cupping her right breast through her bra. His fingers expertly stroked her, as if following a road map drawn long ago and known by heart. He dipped a fingertip into the front of the right bra cup, enticing her nipple to come out and play. She lost her ability to breathe when he fanned her blouse open and took her distended nipple deep into his mouth.

Leah tunneled her fingers through his soft, dark hair, crowding him closer to her chest. He released her nipple, leaving the wet tip bare to the cool night air. One by one, he undid the buttons of her blouse then pulled the delicate fabric out of her waistband. He trailed a hot, wet line down her quivering stomach, then popped open the button to her slacks, immediately covering her exposed flesh with his mouth. Just when she feared he might go farther, he forged a path up to her other breast, laving the nipple through her bra cup, then coaxing it out to join the other where he sucked and licked, nearly driving her insane with the myriad sensations he ignited within her.

J.T. had always known just how to touch her…lick her…stroke her. Was an expert at blowing on the flames of her desire until they grew to a four-alarm blaze. Until it was no longer comfortable for Leah to be in her own skin. Until she felt the world tilt beneath her, everything foreign, remarkable, different.

Leah turned her closed eyes up toward the sky and moaned, the chaos swirling around inside her searing her veins. *Yes,* she wanted to say. *Yes, this is really what I want. I want you, J.T.*

His mouth hesitated on her neck.

"For how long?" he whispered roughly.

Leah blinked her eyes open and tilted her face to look into his. Had she said the words she'd been thinking? Had she told him that this was what she really wanted? She feared she must have.

His hands moved to her hips where he gripped them almost roughly.

Leah licked her parched, well-kissed lips. "I've got to go."

6

DAMN IT, NO MATTER WHAT HE SAID, no matter what he did, J.T. couldn't seem to get through to Leah. And he was filled with panic that he would never make her understand.

"I've got to go," she whispered again, trying to pluck his hands from her hips.

Only a moment ago she'd generously offered her body to him to do with as he wished, and now she shut some sort of invisible door, closing him out again.

He held her still. "Wait. Listen," he said roughly.

Her dark eyes were huge in her beautiful, flushed face as she shook her head. "I can't."

Her words came out as a plaintive cry. J.T. realized that as desperate as he was to get through to her, she was just as desperate to stop him.

He gazed at her, baffled and frustrated and hotter than hell for her.

He abruptly released his grip on her hips and stepped back, giving her the space she needed to leave. But she didn't. She closed her legs and straightened her blouse with trembling fingers, all the time avoiding his gaze. He waited for her to tell him she couldn't see him again. But those words weren't forthcoming, either.

He slid a card from his front shirt pocket. A card on which he'd written the address of the house he was staying at and his cell phone number. He took her hand. She blinked up to stare into his face as he pressed the card into it.

"I'll be there should you change your mind. Come by or call me anytime. Day or night."

He closed her fingers over the card, then gave them a tight squeeze, not wanting to let her go but knowing he had to.

"For how long?"

J.T. squinted at her. Hadn't he just asked the same question of her? Wasn't that the very question that had brought about her change of heart, made her want to leave?

He gave her a brief, sad grin then turned and left her sitting there, not offering up an answer.

Truth was he didn't know how long he was prepared to stay. The job he'd taken on could be done as early as next week. He'd stay on until then. After that, if Leah hadn't contacted him by then...

He didn't want to think about that. Couldn't consider it now.

He rounded the corner of the bar and discovered

a police cruiser driving through the lot. His immediate response was to meld into the shadows of the bar where he couldn't be seen.

No, not yet.

The cruiser slowed near his bike, no doubt taking note of the out-of-state tags. In the far corner of the parking lot near the highway a woman's shout sounded. The officer who was squinting at the Harley turned toward the woman and then the car moved on toward what looked like a domestic argument.

J.T. stayed where he was for the moment, crossing his arms over his chest. He turned his head to see if Leah's car was in view yet and found her standing a few feet behind him, looking at him curiously.

What had she seen? Had she been there when he spotted the police car and ducked into the shadows?

He nodded once in her direction then headed toward his bike, confident that the officer was otherwise occupied with the woman screaming at her date.

THE DRIVE HOME WENT BY TOO quickly. Leah tapped the garage door opener but was forced to leave her car in the driveway when she spotted Sami's bike still upside down on top of newspapers in the garage. She sighed then tapped the opener again to close the door. The door didn't respond. She gathered her school books and her purse and climbed out, deciding to go in through the garage and close the door that way.

It was past eleven and her skin felt cold. Her lips still throbbed with the memory of J.T.'s mouth on hers. Every cell in her body felt brilliantly, liquidly alive no matter how hard she tried to combat the traitorous sensations. It wasn't fair that a man she knew with her head she should have nothing to do with could affect her body so powerfully with his touch.

But no matter how clouded her mind had been with desire, she hadn't missed the way he had avoided being spotted by the police cruiser when she'd gone after him. Certainly those weren't the actions of a man who had nothing to worry about. A year and a half ago she'd wondered at his strange request to be called by his initials rather than his name. And found his vagabond existence more than a little curious. When they were young he talked about being a mechanical engineer. On the occasions that she'd thought about him over the years since then, before he'd come back into her life a year and a half ago, she'd thought he'd be married somewhere, with five kids, be the coach of the baseball team, and probably the football team, too, and be that engineer.

Instead all this time he'd apparently been a dark loner with little more than a motorcycle and a leather bag with a few meager possessions to his name.

Leah pushed the button near the door to the kitchen to shut the garage door and waited while it closed. Could the reason for his behavior be that he was in trouble somehow? Was he wanted for something more than a few outstanding parking tickets?

She'd never considered the possibility before. Had never had cause to. As a judge's daughter she'd been well protected from the criminal element. She'd never known anyone who'd bent the law to the point of breaking it.

Was J.T. in some sort of trouble?

The possibility made her shudder in fear and concern. Not for herself but for him.

She let herself inside the house then locked the door behind her. The light over the stove was on in the kitchen, illuminating her way. She put her class things on top of the small desk built into the counter, hung her keys on a hook then hung her purse next to it.

"Where have you been?" her eleven-year-old daughter's accusatory voice broke the quiet of the night.

Leah slowed her steps, startled by the question. Her daughter was sitting at the kitchen table with a mug of something in front of her, her arms crossed as if she were the adult, Leah the child. A reversal of roles she didn't much care for.

Leah fingered J.T.'s card in the pocket of her slacks and then moved to the refrigerator to pour herself a glass of cold water. "I told you where I went."

"You said you were at Aunt Rachel's. Only Aunt Rachel called and said that you didn't have plans tonight and that she hadn't seen you."

Leah briefly closed her eyes. She hadn't considered that Rachel would call that late. "What are you still doing up? You should have been in bed hours ago."

"I got scared."

Sami hadn't been afraid of anything that went bump in the night since she was two. "Why didn't you call my cell?"

"I did. Only you had it shut off."

Leah swallowed hard. She must have forgotten to switch it back on earlier after canceling her appointment with the counselor.

The telephone rang. Fearful that J.T. might be trying to call her, Leah moved to get it but Sami beat her to it. "It's Dad," Sami said.

Leah stared at her daughter as she spoke to Dan, the last person Leah wanted to think about in that one moment. Her head throbbed with the overload of input, of people demanding her time and attention when all she wanted to do was crawl into bed and bury her head under her pillow until the world started making some sort of sense again.

"Yes, she's home," she half listened to Sami say. "Yes, she's okay. Okay, just a minute."

She held the phone out in Leah's direction.

Leah crossed her arms over her chest, not about to be bullied into doing something she wasn't up to. "Why's your father calling this late at night asking about me?"

Sami flipped her dark blonde hair over her shoulder. "I called him earlier when I couldn't find you, of course."

"Why?"

"Because I was scared."

Leah was growing more impatient with her daughter by the moment. "Tell him I'll talk to him tomorrow."

She wasn't sure who she was more upset with. Her daughter for making her feel guiltier than she already did, or herself for walking straight into that guilt by meeting J.T.

"You tell him." Sami shoved the phone out farther.

When Leah didn't take it, Sami defiantly put the receiver on the counter. "Now that you're home, I'm going to bed. I only hope I can get some sleep."

For long moments Leah stood staring at the telephone, listening as her daughter slammed her door upstairs. What would her ex-husband say if he knew she'd gone to some bar on the outskirts of town to meet a man? Not just any man, but the man with whom she'd had an affair nearly a year and a half ago? The same man that had been the catalyst to the end of their marriage?

No, Dan didn't know J.T.'s name. The way everything had happened, there hadn't been any need to tell him. But even though Dan didn't know, she did. And that's all that mattered in the end. Because as rebellious as she'd ever been in her life, she'd never been a very good liar.

She shakily picked up the receiver.

"Dan, it's late. I'll call you tomorrow."

There was a heartbeat of silence and then he asked, "Are you all right?"

Leah leaned against the wall and rubbed her forehead, trying to untie the knot of tension there. She'd expected her ex-husband to be angry at her for having left Sami alone, accusatory that she'd been out on a Friday night and obviously hadn't been where she'd said she was going. Anything but concerned. His reaction only made her feel worse. "I'm fine. Just tired, that's all."

"All right. Go get some sleep then. I'll talk to you tomorrow."

Leah should have felt relieved but his accommodating tone only made her tense further. "Okay. Thanks. Good night."

She hung up the receiver and stared in the direction her daughter had gone, considering going up after her. Had she really left her cell phone off? She fished the receiver out of her purse. Sure enough, it was still off. She switched it back on then began to put it back into her purse. Changing her mind, she pressed the preprogrammed number for her sister. Rachel picked up in two rings.

"Hey, Rach. I just wanted to call and let you know that I just got home and that everything's all right."

"Why wouldn't it be?"

Leah frowned. "You didn't call here earlier?"

"No. Sami called me. Said something about needing to talk to you about her homework or something but I told her you weren't here."

Sami had called Rachel checking up on her, not the other way around.

Leah stared at the ceiling.

"Is everything okay, Lee?"

"Hmm? Yes. Everything's fine."

She only wished it were.

THE FOLLOWING AFTERNOON J.T. carved the side of a two-by-twelve of rich cherry with a miter saw/

drill, following the newly created curve with his fingers, the grain under his skin smooth and soft. There was something about the physicality of carpentry that drew him in, engaged him. The craft filled four out of his five senses. The sound of the saw, the smell of the wood, the beauty of the grain, the smoothness of the once living object that craved special attention so it might exist for a long, long time to come.

It was nearing 6:00 p.m. and the daylight outside where he was now working hard would soon wane. He'd been at it nonstop since six that morning. He'd taken a brief break to eat the lunch he'd stored in the small refrigerator in the kitchen, but otherwise he'd needed the busyness to keep his mind occupied, needed the labor to drain his body of restless energy.

He finished the length of the wood then powered down the saw and took off his goggles, checking his work with the naked eye. The owner of the house behind him wanted built-in shelving on three walls in the study off the living room. At the rate he was going, he'd be done with the room by tomorrow noon, staining and finishing aside. The day was warm, not hot, but he'd worked up a sweat in the direct light of the sun. Sure, he could have set up his workspace in the shade of the nearby oak or even inside the empty house itself, but he'd wanted to be out in the sun. Feel the heat of it penetrate his skin and warm his bones.

He pulled the handkerchief from his back pocket and dragged it across his forehead, Leah never far from his thoughts. The image of her face was etched into his mind. The taste of her mouth embedded on his tongue. The imprint of her supple breast stamped into his palm. No matter what he was doing, how exhausted he was, or how busy, that was the case. But being so close and not being able to see her made the awareness doubly acute.

He released the clamps holding the wood plank down then stacked it next to the others against the side of the house. He considered what the long day had yielded, then looked beyond to the house itself. A hundred-year-old Victorian that boasted five bedrooms and twelve rooms all told, it was a place he might have imagined himself owning once. It was set back on a full five acres of treed land and was surrounded by farmland beyond that, giving it an open, isolated feel. Homey and private, making it a nice place to raise a large family…and making it the perfect place for him to work. No nosey neighbors who despised him on sight when they saw him on his bike. No traffic that brought by the police every now and again, putting him at risk. Nothing but him and the house and his work.

And thoughts of Leah…

J.T. pulled off his T-shirt and headed inside to wash up before checking the cupboards and the refrigerator for something to make for dinner. He tried not to think about the time. Tried not to think that all it would take was his chopper and ten minutes and he could feast his eyes on Leah without her even knowing he was there.

But that no longer did it for him. When he saw her again, he not only wanted her to know he was there, he wanted her to be the one to seek him out.

He tossed his T-shirt across the side of the downstairs bathtub to dry then turned the faucet on full blast and stuck his head under the strong spray. But the punishing cold water was powerless to stop thoughts of Leah from haunting him. He remembered the expression she wore last night when she'd seen him hiding from the police cruiser. Recalled how she'd told him she couldn't see him anymore and that she wanted him to leave her alone.

When he'd come back to Toledo, he'd told himself he was prepared for her to say that.

Then he'd seen her.

And he'd kissed her.

And that foolhardy belief had deserted him along with any shred of pride.

He wanted Leah. In every way. He wanted to slide between her smooth thighs and feel her slick, hot muscles surrounding him. He wanted to hear his name on her lips. Not his initials, his name. He wanted the scrape of her perfectly manicured nails to leave marks on his back. He wanted to take her to bed at dusk and make love to her until dawn.

He wanted her to be his wife.

He waited for his response to the thought. Prepared himself for shock, disbelief and opposition.

What swept through him instead was a sense of rightness that saturated him all the way to his bone marrow. A knowing that calmed his overworked body, warmed his heart and aroused his need for a woman he would never stop desiring.

He wanted to live with her in a house like this. He wanted to have children with her. He wanted to linger over the Sunday morning funnies with her, go on picnics and long rides. He wanted everything he could have with her.

He knew a moment of pause. This, this epiphany right here, was exactly what he'd been looking for when he'd come back to Toledo. He'd wanted an answer to the emotions constantly rolling inside of him for Leah Dubois Burger. He had expected he might find his emotions had dissipated or even disappeared. Even though he hadn't considered this alternative, he felt remarkably open to it.

Because it was right.

He dried his hands on a towel and wiped his face as he headed out to the kitchen and took a beer out of the fridge. He'd downed half of it before coming up for air and squinting at the seemingly endless stretch of land on the northern side of the house.

He'd never considered taking anyone as his wife. Not difficult to understand considering his past and how he was forced to live now. While he might be free, there was a big difference between the freedom others enjoyed and being on the lam. Mostly because his freedom could be snatched away at any moment and every move he made in populated places put him at risk.

But he'd risk it all for Leah.

But would she have him?

He finished off the beer and dragged the back of his wrist across his mouth. No wasn't an option. Now that he knew what he wanted, he fully intended to have it.

And what he wanted was Leah. And, damn it, he would have her no matter what it took.

He remembered the needy shadow in her eyes last night when he'd lifted her to the pine storage box behind the bar then spread her thighs so he could step between them. He'd intended to take things slowly. To entice her into taking the next step. Make this time different than the times before.

Now he realized he could do that merely by staying.

7

Two days since Leah had last seen J.T. Two nights of tossing and turning in the king-size bed she'd once shared with her husband, waking up with a moan on her lips and her body craving something only J.T. could give her. Forty-eight hours of wading through relentless guilt for having lied to her daughter, her sister and Dan.

She negotiated the SUV through the late-afternoon traffic, the interior of the car warm from the spring sun as she headed for the five o'clock appointment with the couples counselor Colin McKenna. She'd hoped the time away from J.T. would help her clear her mind. Instead she was even more confused than ever.

She reached out to switch on the air conditioner then changed her mind and pushed the automatic window opener instead. Fragrant air rolled into the car, teasing her neat hair and urging her to take a deep breath that filled her body with the newness of spring.

She'd spent more time than she would have liked

in the car over the weekend, driving Sami to soccer practice, piano lessons, the mall and her friends' houses. Normally it would have been Dan's weekend with her, but he'd switched weekends because he was in the eleventh hour of a high-profile murder case and he and his associates needed to prepare for opening statements they'd give today.

Leah was used to the excuse. She'd heard it often enough over the past twelve years. Sami had been disappointed, but she'd gotten over it fairly quickly, especially since Leah always felt she had to make up for her husband's questionable parenting skills and skewed priorities by being a better, more indulgent parent.

Thus she'd forfeited her own time this weekend in exchange for her daughter's happiness.

Which was just as well considering what she would have liked to do with that time.

"Are you well, Leah?" her father had asked the morning before during her weekly Sunday brunch with him and her sister, Rachel. Every now and again Sami joined them, but not often, begging off with an excuse of homework or plans with her friends.

"Fine, Daddy. Busy, but fine." She normally would have wanted to know why he'd asked, but she was learning to steer clear of questions like that in case the person thought it was an open door they'd been invited to walk through.

She couldn't share the truth. She'd hurt her father enough a year and a half ago. He'd accepted Dan as more than his son-in-law, welcoming him instead as a son, and she'd ruined that relationship along with so many others in exchange for a few stolen, empty hours with J. T. West.

Empty...

No, those hours hadn't been empty.

But she had felt achingly empty after he'd left.

She blindly reached into her purse, taking out both her cell phone and the card J.T. had given her. Over the past few days she'd stared at the card countless times, running the pad of her thumb over the blue ink, reading and rereading his phone number and the address where he was staying. But she'd never gotten beyond that.

She came to a red light. She pulled to a stop, her heart thudding an uneven rhythm in her chest as she held the card. Then she entered the number into her keypad and pressed dial. She was putting the phone to her ear when the car behind her beeped, indicating that the light had changed.

She quickly disconnected the call and tossed the phone onto the passenger's seat, her mouth remarkably dry as she continued driving.

God, what had she been thinking?

Long minutes later she pulled into the parking area of the Sylvania medical complex and found a spot near the front of McKenna's office. She didn't spot Dan's Lincoln, which was okay with her because it gave her a few extra moments alone with Dr. McKenna to discuss things she might not have wanted to mention in front of Dan. Today, especially, she was glad for the extra time if only to get her wits about her.

Although the office boasted a receptionist, Colin McKenna was always out in the reception area to greet her and, she guessed, all of his patients.

Patients. God, was she really someone's patient?

"Leah. Good to see you again," he said with a smile. "I'm sorry you couldn't make it last Friday."

She'd forgotten about canceling the lunch appointment last week and hadn't prepared an excuse so she said nothing.

"Why don't we wait for Dan in my office?" Colin opened his door for her then followed her in and closed it after them.

Dr. Colin McKenna was a tall, handsome man who didn't fit her idea of what a marriage counselor should look like. Especially considering that he wasn't and hadn't been married himself. But over the course of the past three months, she'd come to respect his abilities, confided in him things she

wouldn't even tell her sister and trusted that if anyone could help her repair her family, he could.

"Nice weather, isn't it?" He took the chair in the
middle of the room and motioned for her to take one
of the two across from him.

"Hmm? Oh, yes. The weather." Leah nodded as
she sat down and put her purse on the floor next to
the chair. "Spring's always nice."

His eyes narrowed just the slightest bit although
his warm smile remained. "Doesn't sound like your
mind is on the weather."

"No, I guess it's not."

"Anything you'd like to share...you know, before Dan gets here?"

Leah swallowed hard wondering why Dr. Mc-
Kenna seemed to know that she might have some-
thing to say that would be better voiced without
Dan's presence.

"No," she said, chickening out. She offered a
shaky smile. "Full steam ahead, as they say."

"Mmm. So they do."

Leah considered him. There always seemed to be
something just below Dr. McKenna's surface. Almost as if there were something on his mind, something he wanted to share but didn't.

And just like she didn't encourage her father or
sister's curiosity, she didn't encourage Dr. Mc-
Kenna's, either. In her family's case her silence was

for their protection, with Dr. McKenna it was for her own.

Truth was, she was afraid of what lay deep inside her. Was terrified that the same reckless woman who had given in to her desires a year and a half ago would spring forward again, take hold and lead her into even more pain. Not just pain for her, but for everyone around her.

And she couldn't let that happen.

"You're remarkably quiet this afternoon," Dr. McKenna said.

Leah gave a half smile. "Yes, I guess I am." She shrugged. "No complaints. Everything's going smoothly."

"Is it?"

Leah knew that his question was a matter of course. That he was merely encouraging her to go on, expound on her comment. But she couldn't help feeling he was questioning the comment itself.

Or maybe her own subconscious was asking her the question.

A brief knock on the door and a moment later Dan stepped into the room.

"Sorry, I'm late," he said with a grin that was handsome and disarming. He shook Dr. McKenna's hand then leaned down to kiss Leah's cheek, too fast for her to kiss him back. "I didn't miss anything interesting, I hope?"

Dr. McKenna engaged Dan in conversation, allowing Leah to look at her ex-husband, soon to be her husband again. Really look at him again, especially in light of J.T.'s return.

No. J.T. could have nothing to do with what went on in this room. What was going on in her life. She was studying Dan to sort out her own thoughts.

Dan Burger had always been handsome. In high school and college, he had been the football quarterback and team captain. Four years her senior, they'd starting dating when she was eighteen and had met at a Halloween party thrown at his frat house. Almost from the instant they'd been introduced by mutual friends, he'd treated her like she was something special. He'd wooed her and wowed her, taking her to the best restaurants, treating her like a princess to his dashing prince and proposing to her on the night of their third-month anniversary.

If she'd thought things were going too fast back then, she'd ignored it. Truth was, she hadn't been interested in following the same path as her friends who had their lives all planned out like some sort of preprinted restaurant menu. Finish college, go on to graduate school, become engaged, then get married and have children.

Leah had been bored with college and hadn't hesitated to quit and become Dan's wife, over the loud protest of her parents. Within two months of their wedding, she'd become pregnant with Sami and...

And, well, here she and Dan were trying to patch up a marriage that should never have been broken.

"And where does guilt factor into all this for you, Leah?"

Leah blinked, realizing that she'd stayed silent for far too long. Dan and Dr. McKenna had already begun the session without her.

"Pardon me?"

Dr. McKenna smiled at her. "Dan was just saying that he feels guilty for having taken his relationship with you for granted. Expecting you to always be there without any effort from him."

Guilt. That emotion that had threatened to choke off her breath for the past sixteen months.

"I was wondering how you felt about that?" Dr. McKenna prompted, sitting back in his chair.

Leah tilted her chin toward her chest and cleared her throat. "He'd worked hard for where he was...where he is. I never questioned Dan and his commitment to his career."

"Maybe you should have," Dan said quietly.

Leah blinked at him, incapable of words. She'd been married to the man beside her for twelve years yet he seemed like a complete stranger to her. She'd slept in his bed, made his meals, made love with him, bore his daughter, yet all she could think of when she looked at him was she really didn't know who he was.

Or rather, she no longer knew who she was when they were together.

Dr. McKenna leaned forward. "I think what Dan's trying to say, and correct me if I'm wrong, Dan, is that maybe he should have given his marriage the same commitment he made to his career."

Dan nodded, his gaze never leaving Leah's.

She felt that choking sensation again. Only this time she was afraid it wasn't guilt, but suffocation.

"Now then," Dr. McKenna said, "let's move on to what's been happening with Sami during the past week...."

Leah went boneless with relief and she was pretty sure that Dr. McKenna picked up on it.

She fiddled with her watch, sliding it so she could discreetly look at the time. She prayed for help to get her through the next forty minutes.

"Actually," Dan interrupted, sitting earnestly forward, his hands clasped tightly between his knees, "there is something else I wanted to say before we move on to Sami."

Dr. McKenna nodded. "That's okay with me. Is it all right with you, Leah?"

Dan was looking at her with such intensity that she wanted to excuse herself from the room. Instead she forced a smile then nodded.

"I know we've touched on it before, but I'd like for us to set a date for when I might move back to the house. Move back home."

TWO HOURS LATER LEAH WAS sitting in her car, again feeling so outside herself she couldn't seem to concentrate on the simplest tasks. The session had ended, Dan had kissed her on the cheek then gone to pick up Sami for their weekly dinner with Dan's parents. Leah had seen to some errands and done a lot of driving around trying to make sense out of her life, and not having luck. Groceries she really didn't need were packed into the back seat, along with a bottle of wine she really shouldn't have splurged on. The sun was setting, smearing the sky with brilliant oranges and reds. She stared at the horizon, willing herself not to think about anything. Not to remember what had been said during the session. Not to recall that J.T. might still be in town and all it would take was a phone call and he'd be with her within five minutes.

All she had to do was take this one step at a time. Just like she had before. One step, then another, and before too long life settled into a manageable routine and the what ifs and what might have beens fell to the wayside, crowded out by the reality of now and what is. She owed it to Dan, who, miracle of all miracles, wanted to be her husband again. She owed it to Sami, who was having so much trouble adjusting to life with a single parent that her grades were slipping and happiness seemed to be a long-forgotten memory.

And you? What do you need, Leah?

J.T.'s words from last week came back to haunt her. Only she was half afraid they weren't his words, but rather her own.

"This is what I want," she whispered. "I want my life to go back to the way it was. Before…"

Before J.T. Before she'd destroyed everything she'd worked so hard for. Before she'd hurt her husband and child.

And she was moving in that direction with the counseling. Although no date had been set for Dan to move back into the house—her shocked silence when Dan had made his proclamation had prompted Dr. McKenna to step in and say that perhaps they should talk about that next week—there would be soon. And she needed to prepare herself for that. Both mentally and physically.

She'd driven to a greenhouse on the southwestern side of town to pick up a couple of planters of red and white geraniums and now was heading back. Out this far traffic was sparse and dark, elegant houses sat back from the two-lane road.

The Lexus's engine sputtered.

Leah looked down at the gas gauge. She'd filled

up that morning before class and the needle still read nearly full.

Another cough.

She watched the engine light flick on, blinking a bright red at her, indicating the car needed service.

Then the engine died altogether.

Leah checked for traffic behind her, but there was none. She drifted to a stop off on the right shoulder, put the car in Park, then tried to restart the engine. It made a faint ticking sound then went silent again. She'd never run into problems with the high-end automobile. She'd bought it three years ago and didn't have many miles on it and had it serviced like clockwork. She put the car into Neutral then tried to start it again, this time only silence greeting the turn of the key.

She put it in Park again. She could get out and check under the hood, but she didn't know what good that would do because she didn't have any practical knowledge on car repair. She didn't have the faintest idea how to identify what might be wrong, much less fix it, assuming she could identify anything more than where the wiper fluid, the oil and the coolant went. And she had the sneaking suspicion that the problem didn't stem from any of those three.

The sun was slowly sinking down over the horizon. Soon it would be dark and she'd be left out here on this deserted road alone. She shuddered then fished her cell phone out of her purse. Who was the last person she'd called? Rachel. Rachel would come out and keep her company until the auto company showed up.

She hit Redial and the line started to ring as she looked through her purse for her wallet and the auto service's emergency number.

"Hello," a male voice answered.

Very definitely not Rachel.

Leah's heart skipped a beat as she realized that it hadn't been her sister she had called last, but J.T.

She began to pull the phone away to disconnect for the second time that day.

"Leah? Is that you?"

Oh, God, he knew it was her.

"Um, hi," she said, digging the heel of her hand into her forehead. Why had she spoken? Why hadn't she just hung up the instant she'd known it was him?

"Is something wrong?" he asked.

Yes, everything, she wanted to say.

Instead she told him where she was and asked him to come pick her up.

A HALF HOUR LATER LEAH WRAPPED her arms around herself as she watched the tow truck take her Lexus away. The driver had checked under the hood but hadn't been able to tell what the problem was without taking it into the shop. No simple dead battery or loose connection to be found.

Awareness tingled along her skin like a million fingertips, caused by J.T. where he leaned against his bike behind her, his legs crossed at the ankles. She'd asked him to come and he'd come, showing up within five minutes on his motorcycle looking like the best thing she'd ever seen in his snug jeans, scuffed brown boots, white T-shirt and black leather motorcycle jacket.

Strange, but the instant he'd appeared, her confusion had vanished and she'd known a peace that she hadn't felt for a long time.

"Cold?" he asked.

She turned to respond but he stayed her with a hand to her shoulder as he draped his jacket over her. The rich scent of leather combined with the warmth of his skin teased her nose. She knew she should refuse, no matter how chilly the spring air.

"It will be cold on the ride back to your place."

She turned toward him, a strand of her blond hair catching in the corner of her lip, the growing darkness casting his striking face in shadow. "I don't want to go home," she whispered.

8

J.T. LOOKED AT LEAH LONG AND HARD, trying to see
past her wide, dark eyes to the motivation behind
her comment.

"I don't want to go home. Not yet," she said
again, walking toward his Harley.

J.T. stood still for a long moment, watching her
slender silhouette in the waning light. She wore a
pair of cream-colored slacks and a matching short-
sleeve sweater and pumps, looking like a blond-
haired angel in his black leather jacket.

He'd suspected the hang-up earlier in the day had
been her. Only he hadn't expected her to call again.
Or to speak when he'd said her name.

She'd seemed surprised somehow to find him on
the other end of the line. But no more surprised than
he'd been. Particularly when she'd asked him to
come pick her up.

He'd never taken Leah for a ride on his bike. It
had been deep into autumn the last time their paths
had crossed, but that hadn't been the reason why
he'd never ridden with her. No, rather their impa-

tience to be in whatever motel room he'd rented for the night had been to blame for their lack of interest in outside activities.

Leah looked the bike over as if trying to decide how best to get on as she slid her arms into his jacket.

"I get on first. Then you hold on to me to help leverage yourself up," he said.

She nodded, not having met his gaze since making her statement a few moments ago.

Something happened today. Something more than just the breakdown of her car. He sensed it as surely as he sensed he wouldn't be getting his jacket back anytime soon.

J.T. straddled the leather seat of the black 1983 FLH with the shovelhead motor, and waited. A few moments later he felt her hand on his shoulder as she got on behind him. As soon as she was settled into the passenger seat, which sat a few inches higher than his own, he opened up her foot pegs and told her to brace herself on them. Then he reached behind her and grasped her upper thighs, hauling her so that her crotch rested against his back. She gasped, her heat seeming to permeate the thin fabric of her slacks through the thicker denim of his jeans, nearly searing his skin.

"It's safer that way," he said, his words low. "Now put your arms around my waist."

Leah hesitantly placed her fingers against the side of his waist. J.T. caught the limbs and curved them all the way around until her hands rested against his lower abdomen. The softness of her breasts pressed against his back through the opening in his jacket.

J.T. suppressed a groan. How many times had he imagined a moment like this one? Sitting on his bike with Leah behind him? Too many times to count.

He balanced the bike with his legs then released the sidestand, a quick squeeze of the clutch and push of the ignition and the motor growled under them, the seat vibrating from the power of the cycle.

He put on his clear night glasses to protect his eyes then flicked on the headlights, put the bike in gear and pulled out onto the road. "Where do you want to go?" he asked over his shoulder.

There was no answer. For a moment J.T. believed she hadn't heard him. He was about to ask the question again when he felt her cheek against his back.

"Let's just ride."

J.T. squinted into the darkness, the sun little more than a pastel memory on the horizon. He turned left toward the colors, heading west and farther out of the city on the two-lane highway, empty and quiet at this time on a Monday evening, only the occasional house or farm breaking the recently tilled, flat farmland.

"How far do you want me to go?" he asked.

"I'll let you know."

He nodded then found a good, steady pace just below the speed limit and let the Harley hum.

THE COOL NIGHT AIR THREADED through Leah's hair and stung her face as she turned directly into the oncoming wind. She'd never ridden on a motorcycle before and was surprised by the sense of freedom that engulfed her. There was no metal structure or windows around to protect her. Nothing to separate her from the air and nature all around. The seat vibrated beneath her, while between her legs J.T.'s solid body blocked her from taking too much wind. She watched the way his white T-shirt flattened against his muscles and knew he had to be cold. She began to move her hands from around his waist but he caught them in his left hand, preventing the move.

"I'm not going anywhere," she said.

He reluctantly released her and she opened the borrowed jacket, bracketing his waist with the flaps and holding them in place with her arms as she snaked them back around to his front. She felt him relax more against her.

There. That was more like it.

Minutes ticked by as the motorcycle ate up the miles. On the back of J.T.'s bike, it was almost easy for Leah to believe that she was free to do as she wished. Free from the worries of everyday life. Free to ride off into the sunset with him. Free to love him.

She turned her face away from the wind and pressed her cheek against the back of his shoulder again. So strong. So solid. She took a deep breath, detecting the scent of soap and laundry detergent and his own individual musk. She slowly flattened her fingers against the rock-hard wall of his abdomen, and he tensed against her touch under the soft cotton. She felt his left hand grasp her knee and wondered if it was okay for him to do that. To release the handlebars. Then the warmth of his fingers penetrated her slacks and she no longer cared.

The air smelled of things growing, flowers blooming, fresh and new and invigorating. She hugged J.T. tighter, her breasts swelling against the wall of his back, her womanhood growing damp from the contact of her body against his. His grip on her knee increased briefly, then he slid his fingers farther up her thigh until he cupped her bottom. He pulled her closer still, his skin seeming to burn a hole straight through her slacks and branding her flesh.

Leah brushed her nose against his T-shirt then kissed him there. How good it felt to be able to do that. To just place a simple kiss to his back while his motorcycle roared beneath them, steadily eating

up the two-lane road and heading for places unknown.

She continued blindly exploring the muscles of
his abdomen, inching her fingers up toward his
chest. He was even more muscular now than he'd
been back then, if that was possible. All unyielding
steel covered with silken flesh and cotton. She
pointed her hands south and tugged on his shirt until
she freed it from the waist of his jeans then slid her
fingers underneath. She sensed his quick intake of
breath and watched as goose bumps rode up his
forearms.

"Are you cold?" she asked.

He shook his head. "Honey, with you touching
me, I could never be cold."

She smiled against his back and then edged her
fingertips into the waist of his jeans, immediately
finding his arousal pulsing there. She swallowed
hard, the proof of his desire for her even while riding together taking her breath away more than the
speed they were traveling at. She began to draw
away, then discovered she didn't have the strength
to do it. She wanted, no *needed,* to touch him.

She popped the top button of his jeans then
worked her fingers inside the waistband of his briefs,
her skin cool against his hot, rigid flesh. His hand
tightened on her bottom and she cried out, all coiled

tension and pent-up desire. She suspected that if he touched her between her legs she'd climax.

She found a bead of moisture on the knob of his penis. She rubbed it then slipped her hand free so she could taste him, sour and thick against her tongue. After licking her finger, she found his erection again, smoothing her own moisture down the length of him and back up again.

The bike began to slow.

Leah looked around, wondering if they were stopping at a crossroads. But there were no other roads to be seen, no one around at all.

The muscles of J.T.'s legs worked as he brought the bike to a full stop then planted his boots on the ground. Within moments he had shut off the bike, removed his glasses, then got off, not stopping until she was sitting sidesaddle and he was kissing her.

"You drive me...crazy," he whispered harshly, his hands moving faster than she could keep up with as he slid them inside the flaps of the borrowed jacket, pushed her sweater up, then undid the front snap of her bra, freeing her breasts. The cool air hit her bare flesh and she gasped when she felt his hot mouth cover the right tip.

Liquid heat, sure and swift, rushed to pool between her thighs as she curved her legs around his waist and sought purchase against the wide bike seat. He laved and sucked her breasts until she couldn't seem to catch her breath, then he reached around to hold her up so he could rid her of her slacks, leaving her lacy white thong in place.

Leah watched J.T. watching her. She could barely make out the planes of his face in the dark but could feel his gaze blaze a trail from her face to her covered flesh. Balancing herself on one arm, she pulled his zipper the rest of the way down. His erection instantly sprang free, filling her palm as she wrapped her fingers around the heated length. So long…so hard…so thick.

She heard the tearing of a foil packet then moved her hand as he sheathed himself in a condom and rested the pulsing knob against her slick entrance.

It had been so long since she'd had intercourse she knew a moment of pause. More specifically, it had been sixteen months since a man had touched her the way J.T. was touching her now. And it didn't escape her attention that J.T. had been that man.

J.T. cupped her breast then slid his hand down her quivering belly until his thumb pressed on the swollen button, chasing all thought from her mind. His hips bucked forward and he entered her in one, long, breath-stealing stroke.

Leah couldn't seem to draw air into her lungs as J.T. filled her to capacity and beyond. He grasped her hips, pulling her closer to the edge of the seat, forcing her to scramble for balance. Then he slid completely out, the tip of his arousal resting against her clit, then slid back down through her slick, engorged folds to fill her again.

Leah stretched her head back, offering her face to the stars, a moan gathering in the back of her throat. J.T. exited and entered her again, the skin of his legs hot and rough against her inner thighs. She tightened her calves, finding and matching his rhythm.

So good…so right.

Hot, hot chaos gathered tighter and tighter in her belly, making her breasts tingle, her breathing grow more rapid, her womb tremble. She heard J.T. make a sound that resembled a low growl, not that dissimilar from the sound of the Harley. His fingers dug into her bottom as he pressed her even closer to him, rubbing his pubis against hers, his erection buried deep within her, hitting her G-spot dead on.

Leah stiffened at the same time J.T. did, unable to breathe, unable to move, merely able to exist as muscles contracted, heat swirled and bathed and quaked through her body, trapping his hard flesh in her softer, wetter recess.

When their climaxes abated, J.T. buried his face against her neck, holding her close while Leah felt a sob gathering at the back of her throat. He tensed slightly, as if sensing her emotional state. He pulled on his jeans, helped her put on her slacks and fix her bra and sweater, then picked her up from the bike and held her tightly against his chest.

Leah clung to him like he was a rocky island in an ever-moving sea of madness. Somewhere in the back of her mind she was afraid she was holding too tightly, but she couldn't help herself. Having just made love to him, baring her soul and her body to the night air, she could no longer hold in what had for so long needed to come out. She tried to turn away from his gaze, away from where he might see the tears streaking her cheeks, but instead she pressed her face against his neck, loving the smell of him, the texture of his skin against hers.

She wasn't sure what time it was, but knew she should have been home long ago. Dan would be dropping Sami off soon, if he hadn't already. And her ex-husband might be waiting there for her, wanting to share a cup of coffee and talk about what had happened at the counselor's. Discuss the details of his moving back into the house and of their eventual remarriage.

"Leah?" J.T.'s breath stirred the hair next to her ear. "Are you all right?"

She shook her head slightly, refusing to budge from where she was just then. Needing to stay there for as long as she possibly could. "No. I'm not. Nothing will ever be all right again."

AN HOUR LATER JEALOUSY SURE and swift knifed through J.T. as he sat a block up watching Leah see her ex-husband to the door of her house. His fingers tightened against the handgrips as Dan Burger leaned in and kissed Leah's cheek. Leah had her arms crossed in front of her as if to ward off the cold and she turned to look up and down the street, perhaps sensing J.T.'s presence in the shadows.

J.T. knew he should have gone. Should have left as soon as he let her off on the corner a few blocks up. But he hadn't been able to. So he'd found a spot under an old elm tree and stared at Dan Burger's Lincoln Navigator in Leah's driveway until the man finally climbed into the car and backed out.

He watched as Dan passed a few feet to his right, meeting the other man's gaze through the windshield. Then he started his bike and headed in the opposite direction.

He fought to keep his speed at a lawful speed. He knew it was dangerous, his sticking around to see Leah with her ex-husband. He'd gone down this very route before. Even before his affair with Leah a year and a half ago. The first time he'd become involved with a married woman. It was part of the reason he was on the run now, a fugitive from the law. It was the reason he'd left Leah the last time. And it was the reason why he should leave again if he knew what was good for either of them.

He knew it was only a matter of time before his past caught up with him. But he'd always believed it would come by way of a couple of police officers and handcuffs. He'd never once thought he'd live to see history repeat itself.

And no matter the time he and Leah had spent as teenagers during that long-ago summer, that's exactly what was happening. History was repeating itself. He was in love with a woman that wasn't his. She was in love with him.

Only the last time it had happened to him, the woman had ended up dead.

And he had ended up being accused of her murder.

9

"Do you want me to take you to pick up your car?" Dan asked the following day.

Leah had just entered the house after her morning class and was making her way into the kitchen when her ex-husband called. "No. That's not necessary, Dan. The dealership sent me over a loaner this morning. Thanks just the same."

She stared at the now empty kitchen table near the sliding balcony doors. She'd expected recriminations when she'd returned home last night to find Dan and Sami waiting for her while sharing cookies and milk. Instead she'd been welcomed with open arms and they'd made all the right sounds when she'd shared her misfortune. Dan had even gone as far as to ask why she hadn't called him. He could have come pick her up.

She'd told them that the tow truck driver had dropped her off.

Now she said to him on the phone, "You're being awfully attentive today."

"Yes, I guess I am. I don't know. Something Dr. McKenna said yesterday struck home with me."

Dr. McKenna and the session where the theme had been Dan's giving more attention to his career than his marriage.

"That and I...well, I want to come home, Leah. Just say the word and I'll be at the door in ten minutes."

She briefly closed her eyes, not knowing what to say. "Dr. McKenna said it would be best if we discussed that next week."

"I think we need to discuss it now. You and me, face-to-face."

A shudder ran down Leah's back. How was it that she'd forgotten how insistent Dan could be?

"I'd rather we waited," she found herself whispering.

No response.

She cleared her throat and forced cheer into her voice. "How'd everything go in court today?"

A pause then. "Fine. Just fine."

"Good. I'm glad to hear it." She hefted her school bag off her shoulder. "Thanks for calling to make sure everything's all right."

"I'll call you...I mean, is it all right if I call you later?"

She swallowed hard. "Sure. Sure it is." Because they really did need to talk. Not about his moving in. But about possibly putting those plans on the back burner indefinitely.

She disconnected the cordless then neatly dropped it into its cradle. If only everything else about her life were so simple and easy.

But at least she was now getting some sleep.

She placed her class materials on the counter then put on the teapot to boil. She'd felt strangely at peace last night after she'd showered and climbed into bed. Despite that her car had broken down. Despite that she'd come home to find her ex-husband and daughter acting like she'd merely gone out for a quart of milk. And despite that she'd had sex with J.T. She supposed her calm state might have something to do with her no longer fighting her attraction to a man who had stolen her heart a long, long time ago. Or, a small voice in her head prodded, it might be the sexual act itself, the activity and the release of pent-up frustration allowing her to get the rest she sought.

If anything, she faced even larger problems now that she'd accepted that she wanted J.T. and that she was going to have him for however long he was in town. The largest being her reconciliation plans.

She felt tension begin to build again in the crook of her neck and stretched it as she gathered a cup and a tin can of tea bags. She fingered through the options then chose a soothing chamomile. After opening the packet, she put the bag into the cup then went about cleaning up Sami's breakfast dishes.

Her gaze caught on the kitchen clock. Three hours before her daughter returned home from school…

She wiped the counter, telling herself she had bills to pay, course work to finish, a shopping list to make, a living room to sweep.

The next thing she knew she was switching off the teapot, snatching up her purse and heading out the door.

J.T. KNEW THE MINUTE LEAH had pulled up despite that she was driving a different car, that the miter saw was droning away and that he had his back turned toward the driveway. He could tell because of the way his body vibrated like some sort of divining rod whenever she was near.

He shut off the saw and glanced at his watch. Just before twelve thirty. She would have just knocked off class at the university, stopped by the house, then made her way straight out here.

He lifted his goggles so they rested above his brows then turned to watch her get out of the car. She had on a pair of tan slacks today matched with a white blouse. He wondered if she had any red in her closet. Something, anything with any color.

He also wondered if she had anything on her mind other than sex. And despite his own clamoring want of her, it bothered him to think she might be there just for sex.

She advanced on him, her dark eyes all hot desire, her breasts pressing against the front of her blouse, her movements determined and undeniably sexy. She stopped in front of him, put her purse down next to the saw, then reached up and pulled off his goggles and started kissing him.

Good Lord, what this woman did to him. He was standing there drenched in sweat, his muscles aching, his stomach empty from not having eaten since the day before, and Leah made him forget all of that with one hungry kiss.

"Hello to you, too," he murmured, cupping her shoulders and pulling her slightly away.

He glanced toward the road a hundred feet away to find one of the neighbors passing in a truck.

"Aren't you worried about being spotted?" he asked.

"The car's a loaner."

J.T. suspicions of her motivations amplified. He'd much rather she'd have said she didn't care who saw her. That she wanted him and that was the beginning and the end.

She grabbed his hand and started leading him into the house.

J.T. watched her curvy little bottom in the neat slacks, wondering what kind of underwear she had on today. He decided she had to be wearing one of those thongs again because he couldn't detect any panty lines.

Leah stopped just inside the door and looked around. He'd rolled up his sleeping bag in the corner to keep it free of sawdust and out of the way. She instantly headed in that direction.

J.T. held fast. "Can a guy catch a shower first?"

She turned toward him while still holding his hand and backing toward the sleeping bag. "But I want you to be dirty, Josh." Her expression made it clear what she meant.

She'd used his name again. J.T. swallowed hard, staring at her passion-filled face; the way her eyes were so dark with her pupils dilated; the plump, moist stretch of her bottom lip; the flush of color on her pale cheeks. Her blond hair was shiny and neat and combed, her makeup applied just so. And he knew an overpowering desire to mess it all up.

He reached out and tangled his fingers in the strands over her right ear, piling it up until it sat on top of her head, then he did the same with the other side until her hair was a tangled, unruly mass.

Then he leaned in to do what he could about the blasted makeup.

When he kissed her, Leah made a whimpering sound that set his blood to simmering, making him forget about the work that needed to be done, that it was the middle of the day and that she'd very obviously come out just for sex. He found the top of her blouse with his fingers and gave a tug, taking some satisfaction in hearing a couple of buttons pop off and scatter across the unfinished wood floor. She followed suit by ripping at his T-shirt.

They both tugged and pulled and opened until they were naked in the curtainless room, and trying to open the sleeping bag while still kissing.

Damn, but she tasted good. Too good. Like toothpaste and sunshine and desire, clean and bright and sexy as all hell. As soon as the bag was ready, he spread her across it, watching as her hair spilled over the navy blue fabric, her slender thighs spread, baring all to his hungry gaze. J.T. groaned and spread her even farther, fastening his mouth directly to her clit, drinking from her honey depths like she was the fountain of life. He felt her hands clutching his hair, heard her deep moans, but could focus on little more than laving her, running his tongue through her shallow, swollen folds of flesh, lapping up her sweet juices and suckling the bit of soft flesh at the apex. He drew it deep into his mouth and swirled his tongue around and around until her grip on his hair increased and she cried out, her delectable body dissolving into a seemingly never-ending wave of spasms.

She shivered as he licked her one last time. He

took in her fevered appearance. Her trembling lips. Her wide, drowsy eyes. The deep flush of color on her creamy skin. He sheathed himself with a condom, then abruptly turned her over and drew her to her knees until her plump backside pointed up toward him, her breasts swaying underneath. Leah gasped. A gasp that turned into a low, even moan as he fit himself against her dripping portal then slammed in to the hilt.

Last night he had been eager but gentle. Today he was filled with a strange agitation, a frustration that had little to do with sex and more to do with the woman whose only interest in him appeared to have to do with sex. He withdrew and slammed into her again, drawing out another long moan and watching as her flesh shuddered against his onslaught. He gripped her lush hips, watching as his dark, dirty fingers indented her clean, pale flesh. Then he slammed into her again…and again, his movements manic and domineering, his intent almost to hurt her rather than to bring her pleasure. And aware that by doing so, he was bringing her even more pleasure.

But he wouldn't allow himself to hurt her. It took all he had to rein his wild aggression. He collapsed on top of her, out of breath, his body drained and drenched in sweat. Realizing she was having trouble breathing, he rolled off to lie flat on his back, drap-

ing an arm across his brow to shield his eyes as he
stared at the ceiling.

He watched as she straddled him, holding herself
high and proud, the peaks of her breasts hard and
knotted. He'd succeeded in messing up her makeup
and hair, but she emerged even more beautiful, un-
bearably so, almost untouchable. J.T. reached out to
cup her cheek. She turned her face into his palm and
sank her teeth into the skin there even as she lowered her sweet body over his straining erection.

He gritted his teeth and stretched his neck, so
close to climax. Through a slit in his eyelids, he
watched Leah's pink, swollen flesh move up and
down over his glistening shaft, her breasts jiggling,
her arms braced against his shoulders, her face a
portrait of needy passion. He shifted her arms from
his shoulders, forcing her to reach behind and brace
herself against his thighs. The new position slowed
her strokes and allowed him an even better view of
their bodies melding then parting then melding together again. Outside the sun began its afternoon
move toward the horizon and shafts of light slanted
in through the windows, bathing Leah in a golden,
surreal light. Her eyes were closed, her mouth
bowed as she moaned and moved slowly up and
down his thick erection.

J.T. grasped her thighs, parting her farther, then
pressed both thumbs against the sensitive flesh he

uncovered. Almost instantly Leah cried out, her body freezing as she gave herself over to her second orgasm.

But J.T. didn't allow himself the release. Instead he gritted his teeth to ward off his climax, content to watch her. Or not so much content as preoccupied. He loved claiming her sweet body. Loved giving her orgasm after orgasm.

But it was her heart he was after.

And he was afraid he'd never reach it.

AN HOUR LATER LEAH LAY on her stomach on the sleeping bag, her head turned away from J.T., completely boneless, a blink away from dozing off. The sun through the window felt warm against her damp back, her sex throbbed and pulsed, filled with blood and swollen almost to the point of pain.

One minute she'd been facing an afternoon filled with house chores and homework, the next J.T. was between her thighs giving her an exquisite pleasure no other man had ever given her before.

She nudged her watch around her wrist and glanced idly at the time.

J.T. moved beside her. She glanced to find him getting up.

"Josh?" she said quietly.

He glanced at her as he gathered up her things and tossed them onto the sleeping bag, then plucked up his jeans from the floor. His face was drawn into hard lines, his eyes dark and unreadable.

"Where are you going?"

"The bathroom."

He turned and walked toward a room down the hall. She winced as the door closed and locked behind him.

Leah rolled over to stare at the ceiling, vaguely aware that her stomach was growling. She, the perfect hostess, the mother hen, the one who always made sure no one left her house with an empty stomach, hadn't even thought about making a couple of sandwiches, or picking up fried chicken on her way out. Sex had been all that was on her mind. And sex is what J.T. had given her. And then some. She swallowed hard, wondering if she was going to be able to walk properly when it was time to go.

She pushed herself up into a sitting position and idly put her panties back on, followed by her pants and her bra. She was just shrugging into her blouse when the bathroom door opened and J.T. reappeared, his hair wet, his dark, shirtless skin glistening with droplets of water, his jeans fastened. He stopped near her, but rather than touching her as she'd hoped he'd been about to do, he reached beyond her to collect his work boots. He put them on without socks and grabbed a black T-shirt from a duffel bag in the corner then headed outside without saying a word.

Leah blinked after him. Her intention had been to go to the bathroom and fix herself up. Instead she stalked outside after J.T. Only what she saw made her steps falter. J.T. was standing near his workbench, but it wasn't his work he was concentrating on but rather the state highway patrol car passing on the road a quarter of a mile away.

She knew a moment of fear.

J.T. wore the same stony, wary expression she'd seen last week when the police car had passed through the parking lot of the bar. If there were any shadows around, she was sure he would have stepped into them. As it was, he appeared ready to bolt at a moment's notice.

"What kind of trouble are you in?" she whispered.

He appeared surprised by her presence, staring at her through the plastic safety goggles much as he had stared at the highway patrolmen who had slowly moved on down the road. He didn't answer her question and she realized she hadn't expected him to. But that didn't mean she was giving up, either.

"What's going on that you're not telling me?" she asked, reaching up to push the goggles from his eyes.

J.T. snatched them completely off, his eyes glittering dangerously under the midday sun. "I should be asking that question of you, Leah. You got what you came for. Don't you have your life to get back to now?"

Leah winced, feeling like she'd just been slapped across the face. "I don't deserve that."

"Don't you?" he asked with a cocked brow. "I've been trying to talk to you for the past week, but conversation is never on your agenda. The only thing you seem interested in is screwing."

She winced again, looking back at the empty road.

"What? Don't you like that word, Leah? Well, you'd better get used to it because what we did in there, and what we did last night, was screw. Pure and simple."

"Maybe to you," she whispered, backing away from him.

"Oh? Then tell me what you think it is when a woman comes after you, no words, no conversation, and seduces you into sleeping with her." He stepped closer, erasing the distance she was putting between them. "Do you call it making love?"

She swallowed through the thickness in her throat, the sensation of being suffocated rolling over her. "That's not fair."

"Yeah, well, join the club. Because I'm not finding much about what's going on between us fair, either.''

He looked beyond her to the road. Through the cloud of pain he'd just inflicted on her, her suspicion grew that J.T. was in some kind of trouble. ''Are you on the run, J.T.? Is that why you don't want me to call you by your real name? Is that why you left here like a ghost, leaving no forwarding address? Without even saying goodbye?''

He didn't say anything for a long moment. Instead he put his goggles back on and readied his saw.

''I think you'd better go now, Leah.''

She nodded. Yes. She probably should. There was so much about standing there in front of him, listening to him question her reasons for coming to see him, wondering about his safety, that made her feel sick inside.

Besides, Sami would be home from school.

She realized she was caught between two irreconcilable worlds and as she stared at J.T.'s handsome face, the ache in her chest sharpened to a knifepoint.

She turned and he grasped her wrist in his strong hand. ''Tell me, Leah. Have you even once considered a place for me in your future?''

She stared at him unblinkingly. She might have once. A year and a half ago.

But then he'd left, destroying whatever secret hopes she may have nursed.

The memory of that pain swirled with today's confusion and prompted her to lie. "No," she whispered.

He released her wrist and she hurried toward her loaner car, her heart beating so quickly she half wondered if she might go into cardiac arrest. She had to try twice to open the door then finally she was inside and backing out onto the road, leaving J.T. standing right where he was when she'd first pulled up.

10

LEAH CUT CARROTS AND ONIONS at the island counter in her bright and cheery kitchen that neither cheered nor brightened her at all, her movements automatic, staccato, much as she'd conducted all activities since leaving J.T. standing staring after her the day before last. Over forty-eight hours had passed since then, but it might as well have been five minutes. His words still stung. Her body still ached both from his attention and for his attentions.

And her life hadn't improved one iota since.

Sami stomped through the kitchen, all evidence of her good nature three nights ago when her father was there having evaporated, apparently stowed away until the next time Dan was present.

"I don't know why Dad couldn't come to dinner," Sami said, dropping a small basket of dirty clothes she'd brought from her room at Leah's request on the floor then crossing her thin arms over her T-shirt–covered chest. "I mean, it's not like we don't have enough food. You fix enough to feed my entire fifth-grade class."

Leah kept her attention on the vegetables lest she lop off a finger and accidentally toss it into the mix. "We've already talked about this, Sami." Again and again and again. "Your relationship with your father is outside my relationship with him. If your plans involve the house, then they involve me. And since you didn't consult me before inviting him over..."

"You get to say no," Sami finished. She threw her hands up into the air then let them drop back to her sides with a loud slap. "But this is his house, too. He bought it."

Leah was forced to put the knife aside, not so much because of the risk it presented to her, but of the risk it was increasingly presenting to her obnoxious daughter. She spread her hands flat against the counter and counted backward from ten. "Sami," she said in warning.

As it turned out, she and Dan had jointly bought the house. She'd put down the hefty down payment using trust fund monies and cash gifts her parents and her family had given her on their wedding day. And Dan's payments since then and until just prior to their divorce about equaled that amount. She'd been keeping up the mortgage payments since with a little help from proceeds from her mother's life insurance policy and quarterly returns from an investment she'd made in a small local business five years ago. All child support payments she put into the trust fund she'd set up for Sami when she was born. She and Dan had agreed that until Sami turned eighteen—barring any mutual understanding between them prior to that date—the house would remain in Leah's possession. When it was sold, a court arbitrator would decide on equitable distribution of the proceeds.

Try explaining all that to her eleven-year-old daughter.

Especially considering that no one, including her sister, Rachel, knew about her investment in the Women Only store just this side of the Michigan border near Raceway Park. She played silent partner in the lingerie shop, and the managing partner was trying to get her to franchise on the opposite side of town.

"Do your laundry, Sami."

Her daughter kicked the basket, sending the clothes tumbling out over the floor. "You do the stupid laundry. That's your job. Dad says it is." She glared at her, as if daring her to deny it. "You don't do anything all day anyway."

In that moment it was difficult to remember that Sami had once been a happy, cheery little girl always smiling, always laughing, bringing sunshine wherever she went. The baby who had rarely cried. The toddler who had learned to walk fast and to talk even faster and who loved to be read to. The five-year-old who used to run home from school to show Mommy the new picture she had drawn so they could use magnets to put it on the refrigerator. The eight-year-old who had cried in her arms the first time a boy had called her a word she didn't understand.

Then, overnight it sometimes seemed, Sami had changed. It was normal, the child psychologist she had consulted with after her and Dan's separation had told her. All she needed to do was keep reassuring Sami that she wasn't to blame for her and her father's breakup.

Unfortunately it seemed that by telling her daughter that so often, Sami had come to understand that *Leah* was to blame. And took an evil kind of pleasure in reminding her that she'd never forgive her for it.

"Pick up your clothes, Sami, and put them in the washer."

So much hostility. She watched the eleven-year-old angrily shove her clothes back into the basket, piece by piece, make a loud sound of frustration, then disappear into the hall leading to the laundry room.

Leah honestly couldn't say where her daughter had picked up the behavior. She and Dan had never argued or raised their voices to each other, either in or away from their daughter's presence. Their separation had been amicable if frosty, as had been their divorce, no bitter recriminations, no unreasonable demands made by either party. Quite simply, Leah had told her husband she was in love with another man and he had reluctantly accepted it.

J.T.'s image, as large as the Swiss Alps and twice as breathtaking, emerged in her mind and her palms grew damp.

She'd forgotten she'd told Dan about J.T. No, she hadn't used his name. Dan had never even asked who he was. When she'd come home late one night, he'd asked where she'd been and she'd told her husband about a man in her life and that she wanted a divorce. He had moved his things into the downstairs study and agreed to give her one.

Then the next day had come with no sign of J.T. Then another. Then a week. Dan had moved into a condo. They had gotten a legal separation. Then a month had passed by without word from J.T. and she'd had to accept that she probably wouldn't be seeing him again.

She'd continued with the divorce, of course. It had been too late to turn back then.

Then during Christmas last year Dan had finally asked about the man she'd divorced him for and she had told him he was no longer in the picture and hadn't been for a long time. And Dan had asked her to consider remarriage.

She'd seen no reason to refuse him. He was the father of her child. They were friends. And she had loved him once and could probably love him again.

Then J.T. had come back.

The oil in the pan on the gas burner began to burn. She opened her eyes, surprised she had closed them, and removed the pan and shut off the flame.

"Mom!" Sami's voice peeled from the direction of the laundry room.

Leah wiped her hands on a towel and went to go see which of her daughter's clothes she had ruined this time. Only when she pushed open the door she found Sami standing ankle deep in water.

She quickly directed her daughter from the room away from risk of electrocution then reached across and shut off the water from the main pipe.

"Dad's going to hit the roof when he finds out what this is going to cost," Sami said.

Screw Dad, Leah wanted to say.

Instead she walked into the kitchen and picked up the phone, dialing the only person she wanted to come help her.

J.T. STOOD ON LEAH'S DOORSTEP, tools in hand, wondering what the hell he was doing there. He'd spotted her Lexus in the driveway when he'd parked up the block so he guessed she'd had the car fixed. Somehow it bothered him knowing she was going on about her normal, day-to-day life without including him in those activities.

That she was suddenly including him now...

The door swung open to reveal Leah's eleven-year-old impish daughter, Sami.

Like so many things in their relationship, Leah hadn't talked about her daughter much. He suspected because they didn't get a chance to talk about much of anything at all. But judging by the wary expression on the girl's face, she wasn't inclined to like him. In fact, it appeared she might even hate the world at large.

"Who are you and what do you want?" she asked, confirming J.T.'s suspicions.

"Sami!" He heard Leah's voice from inside the house. "Is that any way to greet a guest?"

The girl looked over her shoulder. "It's not a guest, it's some guy selling stuff."

Leah appeared behind her daughter, putting her hands on her shoulders and squeezing a little hard given the way Sami winced. "Sami, say hello to Mr. West."

Sami said something under her breath that might have been considered a greeting. "If you're hoping for dinner, you're out of luck. Mom doesn't want any dinner guests tonight."

Leah stared at her daughter then turned her around and pointed her toward the stairs. "Say goodbye to Mr. West then go up to your room until I call for you."

"Goodbye, Mr. West."

The girl took the stairs two at a time and moments later a door slammed. Leah jumped.

J.T. stared after the little hellion on wheels.

"I never quite get used to that," Leah said with a shaky smile.

She motioned for him to come inside and he did. He couldn't help noticing the way she looked out to see if anyone was watching before closing the door.

J.T. glanced around the foyer. "I imagine you did a lot of door slamming when you were her age."

Leah blinked at him as if surprised by his comment. Then her brows drew together. "You know, I think I probably did."

J.T. stood in the two-story foyer, glancing around at the crystal chandelier, the rich wood paneling and the parquet floors. He knew exactly what kind of money it took to make a house look like this. And it was money he wouldn't be coming into anytime soon.

He cleared his throat, at odds with the woman and the house she lived in.

He'd always known Leah was high maintenance. When they were teenagers she'd always worn the latest, most popular brand of jeans, had spent hours getting ready for an event that wouldn't last half as long, and her family had rented—perhaps even owned—the four-bedroom cabin they'd stayed in the month of August.

By contrast, he'd always worn what had fit him and he and his father had stayed in the cramped trailer that had served as their home year-round.

But somehow when he touched Leah, all that slipped away, leaving a man and woman and their powerful attraction to each other.

An attraction that dimmed not at all standing in the foyer of the house she'd once shared with her husband.

Damn, she looked good. And he wasn't talking about the products in her hair that made it shiny and straight. Or the expensive outfit she wore. He was drawn to the warm glow of her skin, the clearness of her eyes and the tightness of her attractive body.

He caught her curious gaze and realized she was probably thinking the same thing he was.

No, their attraction to each other hadn't changed. But what he allowed himself to do in connection to it…well, that had changed completely.

"You said you had a leak you needed help with?" he said quietly, forcing his attention away from her and to the house.

"Oh, yes! Sorry." She led the way down the hall toward the kitchen. "The laundry room's this way."

He followed, watching the way her bottom swayed under her beige slacks. Did she no longer own a pair of jeans? It wasn't too long ago that he remembered that's all she wore. Then again, maybe it was a lifetime and a different person ago.

She pushed open a door. "I don't know what could have happened. I've mopped up most of the water. There was a good three to five inches of it in here."

J.T. crouched down and checked the integrity of the flooring. "Do you have a basement?"

"Half."

"I'll have to go down afterward to take a look. Make sure there's no damage."

She nodded.

J.T. tried to ignore how much he wanted to forget about what had passed between them two days ago and just touch her. She smelled good and he knew she'd taste even better. In contrast, he'd been working outside all day and was coated in sweat and sawdust and probably smelled like yesterday's meatloaf. He opened his bag and took out his tools then pulled the washing machine out to have a look. Realizing she was still standing in the doorway, he glanced her way.

"I don't suppose you need my help, do you?"

she said quietly, desire burning bright in her dark eyes.

He shook his head, not trusting himself to speak.

"Okay. I, um, I'll just be out in the kitchen finishing dinner." She started to walk away. "Oh, and despite what Sami said, you're more than welcome to stay."

J.T. stared evenly at her, trying to figure out the reason behind the invite to dinner, but Leah had already left the doorway, her steps sounding on the wood plank flooring as she walked away.

"You may want to check with your daughter first," he said to himself. "I think she'd have a thing or two to say about my staying."

He took out a monkey wrench and gave the pipe a tap. He hadn't expected the exercise to produce anything but was surprised when the pipe shifted, revealing that it had been cut in two.

He sat back on his ankles and considered it, then looked around the room. Odd.

He pushed to his feet then stepped back out into the kitchen. His steps slowed when he found Leah with her back to him, adding chopped vegetables to a pan on the stove. No matter how many times he saw her, she took his breath away. But this was the first time he'd seen her at anything domestic aside from the chores she did outside like take out the garbage or work in the garden.

He'd grown up without a mother so the only sight he'd gotten of someone in the kitchen was of his father, and his culinary skills had been limited to putting in and taking out frozen dinners from the conventional oven, then, later, the microwave. Every now and again he'd gotten ambitious and boiled bratwurst in beer, or made a throat-burning chili, but otherwise their meals had come from the freezer or a can.

Watching Leah now made him feel...strange. Like he was seeing something he wasn't entitled to be seeing. The sight of her cooking from scratch struck him as overly intimate. Ranking right up there with watching her take a bath, which was something else he'd like to see.

Leah finished what she was doing then jumped when she turned to find him standing on the other side of the island. "J.T., you startled me."

He eyed the way a strand of her silky hair stuck against her elegant throat and longed to move it out of the way...with his mouth. "I need to pick up some supplies. I'll be back in fifteen minutes."

Her gaze had drifted from his eyes and rested against his chest. She looked back up into his face. "Okay. The front door's open so just walk back in."

"I'd rather not."

"Sure. Okay. Just knock and I'll make sure *I* get it this time."

J.T. walked out of the room.

Leah collapsed against the counter, her heart going a million miles a minute as she listened to the front door close behind J.T.

She didn't know why she'd reacted the way she had. Turning around and seeing him standing there in his jeans and a T-shirt had seemed...so right. His jeans had born evidence of his work that day, but she guessed he must have cleaned up and changed his T-shirt before coming out, his dark hair still damp at the ends.

"Is he gone?"

Leah blinked her daughter's face into focus. She frowned and continued on to the sink where she cleaned up the cutting board. "He went to get some supplies."

Sami rolled his eyes. "You would have thought he'd have them with him seeing as he does it for a living."

"He doesn't do it for a living. He's a friend doing a favor for me."

She ignored her daughter's accusatory stare as she put the cutting board away then checked the roast in the oven. Judging it just about done she grabbed an oven mitt and took it out to cool.

"Why didn't you call Dad?"

Leah pretended she wasn't affected one way or the other by her daughter's questioning. "Because your dad will be the first to admit he doesn't know a thing about plumbing.''

''You never know. Maybe he's taking a class or something. Like you.''

Leah highly doubted her daughter even knew what classes she was taking. Probably wasn't the slightest bit interested in knowing that she was studying to finish her business degree. A degree she hadn't gotten twelve years ago because she'd gotten pregnant with Sami.

''Maybe I should call him,'' Sami said.

Leah stared at where her daughter had picked up the phone. ''Put it down, Sami.''

''Why? I'm sure—''

She took the phone from the eleven-year-old's hand and hung it back up. ''J.T.'s already looking into it. Don't you think it would be rude if he came back with the parts to find someone else fixing it?''

''I think you're rude,'' Sami said.

''I thought I told you to go up to your room until I called you?''

''I heard him leave.''

She said ''him'' as though she was talking about a snake. ''Well, he's coming back so you'd better hurry upstairs. You know, so you don't catch cooties or something equally horrifying.''

Sami rolled her eyes but to Leah's surprise she

did crack a bit of a smile. "Cooties is so kindergarten, Mom."

She smiled back. "Then whatever it is they call what you don't want to catch nowadays."

"Herpes?"

"What do you know about herpes? Sami?"

But her daughter had already left the room. This time, thankfully, she hadn't slammed her door.

AN HOUR LATER J.T. CAME OUT of the laundry room. Leah and her daughter were sitting at the dinner table though neither of them had anything on their plates.

"All done," he said, gesturing toward the sink. "Do you mind?"

"No, no. Go right ahead."

He flicked on the faucet and began cleaning up. Leah had gotten up from the table and stood behind one of the chairs. When he was done, he dried his hands with a couple of paper towels then turned toward them.

"Sami and I were hoping you would join us for dinner," she said.

J.T. squinted at the girl sitting at the table pretending not to be paying attention though he was pretty sure he saw her ears twitching from listening so hard.

How many times had he envisioned a situation

like this? He, Leah and her daughter sharing a meal at a dinner table?

The only problem was that nothing had been resolved between them. They pretty much stood where they had two days ago, which was nowhere, no matter how much he'd like to believe otherwise.

"Sorry," he said, picking up his bag. "But I've already got other plans."

Both Leah's and Sami's gazes flew to his face. In Leah's eyes he read shock and disappointment. In Sami's he spotted relief.

"Um, okay," Leah said, appearing not to know what to do with her hands as she released the back of the chair. "I'll see you out then."

"Make sure you give him a good tip," Sami called after them.

He caught Leah's wince.

"Fortunately she doesn't have a clue what kind of tip I'd ask for," J.T. said as they made their way down the hall toward the door.

They stopped in the foyer and Leah faced him, apparently not knowing how to respond to his leaving. Finally she said, "Thanks, you know, for coming over so quickly. For fixing the washer."

"I didn't fix the washer—I fixed the pipe. Which, I have to tell you, looks like it may have been cut."

"I don't understand. Cut? As in purposely?"

He nodded then pushed his hair back from his

face. He was overdue for a haircut and it kept falling over his brow. "My guess is a hacksaw."

"Sami?"

He shook his head. "No. She doesn't have enough strength to cut through solid pipe." He hoisted his tool belt to his shoulder. "Anyway, I just thought you should know."

He opened the door and walked out onto the steps.

"Josh?"

He turned back toward her, his stomach tightening every time she used his real name.

"I'm...sorry about what I said the other day."

He looked down at his feet and nodded. "Yeah. Me, too."

J.T. turned and walked away, unsure of what else to say. Unsure if there was anything else to say.

11

As much as Leah longed to go to J.T.'s later that night, she denied herself the opportunity. Given the words that had passed between them, and the words that hadn't, everything was still too fresh, too raw, to be poked at again so soon. What he'd said the other day had been on target. She owed him more than she could offer him just then. Her body might be his, but where was her heart? She loved him beyond reason, but was coming to fear that wasn't enough. Not when so many other balls hovered in the air above her head, dependent upon her dubious juggling abilities to keep them aloft.

But whatever else was going on, she knew that if she went to his place, they would end up on his sleeping bag, giving themselves over to the passion that burned through their veins. And aside from bone-deep physical satisfaction, that would accomplish nothing but the deepening of the confusion between them.

She dropped Sami off for her usual study group at seven then drove to her sister's instead. Although she questioned the wisdom of her actions when she found Rachel knee-deep in bridal bouquet models and sampling several different types of wine.

Rachel closed the door after Leah and gave a loud hiccup.

"Just the person I need to see," Rachel said, swaying slightly as she led the way into the living room, the bit of wine in her glass sloshing and threatening to spill out onto the new area rug.

Leah looked around the recently renovated house her sister had bought a few months ago in the Harmony area. Every time she visited Rachel had added something else, and this time was no exception. Sprigs and arrangements of dried flowers were artfully placed here and there, giving the place a homey, feminine feel.

"Here, try this." Rachel had poured a healthy finger of red wine into another crystal wineglass and handed it to Leah. "I think this is the one I want for the reception."

Leah sniffed the bouquet of the wine, then swirled it, checking for sediment before giving it an experimental taste.

She nearly spit the poor excuse for wine right back out. "It tastes like vinegar."

Rachel threw back her head and laughed. "That's what Gabe said." She shrugged and added more of the same wine to her glass. "That's why I think it's the one I should go with,'' she said, her expression disgruntled.

Leah caught her sister when she might have tripped over a bouquet of pink roses and white baby's breath. ''I think you've fried your taste buds, little sister.''

Rachel allowed her to steer her toward one of the two couches that sat face-to-face beside the fireplace. ''Hazards of the job, I guess.'' She waved her hand, seeming to take extra interest in the action as she stared at her fingers moving in front of her face. ''You know, it's a lot of work being a bride.''

''Tell me about it.'' Leah sat next to her sister and covertly poured the contents of Rachel's glass into her own, then filled Rachel's with water from a bottle sitting nearby. ''Just remembering my wedding makes me want to swear that I'll never get married again.''

She caught her words, just then realizing that she was not only planning on marrying again, she was going to do it to the same man.

Rachel picked up her glass, making a face when she realized it was water. She reached for the wine bottle and Leah took it from her. ''Hey, that's my little helper.''

''Yes, well, it's time the little helper called it a night.'' She put the bottle on the other side of the couch on the floor where Rachel would inevitably forget about it in a few moments. "Now, tell me what's going on. Is it the house? Are you and Gabe still debating where you're going to live?"

Rachel wrinkled her nose. The action when combined with her short hair made her look all of sixteen. "No. I mean, yes, we are, but that's not what's bothering me tonight."

She picked up one of the bouquets and plucked at the fake flowers, presumably to straighten them. "Do you like this one? Gabe hates it. It's my favorite."

Leah tried to hold back a smile but failed. Rachel frowned at her. "That's the problem? The flowers?" Leah asked.

Rachel dropped her arms and the bouquet flopped into her lap. "That's the problem. The wine's the problem. The color of the bridesmaids' dresses is the problem." She leaned closer, which put her flush against Leah. "By the way, I think you'd look great in red at the wedding. You never wear red anymore. Why is that?"

Leah wasn't comfortable with the question so she avoided it. "So you and Gabe aren't seeing eye to eye on the arrangements then."

Rachel stuck out her tongue and made a loud raspberry sound. "Eye to eye? He's lucky to have any eyes left after today. I mean, here I am, trying to run my legal office when I'm not in council chambers, and working my butt off to try to put this wedding together and he just swoops down and pooh-poohs everything I choose. 'You handle the arrangements, baby, I trust your judgment.''' She snorted in an indelicate manner then appeared shocked the sound had come from her. ''It's a good thing he's so damn good in bed or I'd call the whole thing off.''

Leah put her hand over her mouth to keep from smiling.

''Are you laughing? You're laughing at me, aren't you?'' Rachel accused.

Leah shook her head.

Her sister gave a long sigh, put her feet up on the coffee table between the two couches then sank into the cushions. ''That's all right. If I were you I'd probably be laughing at me, too.''

She sipped the water from her glass and considered Leah over the rim. ''So what are you doing here, anyway? Don't you have a daughter to raise? An ex-husband to reconcile with?''

Leah kicked off her shoes and mimicked her sister's actions by putting her feet up on the coffee table and slumping against the cushions. ''Is that the way you see my life, too? A list of tracks?'' She picked up the bouquet from Rachel's lap. ''That's the second time I've heard that today. 'Doing my laundry is part of your job,' is I think how Sami put it.''

"Did you make her eat the laundry?"

Leah smiled and turned her head in her sister's direction. "No. But I will admit the thought crossed my mind.''

Rachel leaned closer so that their heads were touching. "Sounds like your day was pretty crappy, as well.''

"Crappy about covers it.'' She shifted slightly. "Rachel, what do you think about Dan?''

Leah wasn't entirely sure where the question had come from, but now that she'd asked it, she was curious what her sister's answer would be.

"How do you mean?'' Rachel asked carefully. "What do I think of Dan as a man in general? Or as your husband?''

"Both.''

Rachel reached for the bouquet and Leah gave it to her, watching as her sister straightened the silk blossoms. "I don't know. He's okay, I guess.''

"Just okay?''

Rachel shrugged. "I remember the first time you brought him home to meet Mom and Dad.'' She rubbed her nose with the back of her hand. "Mom said something along the lines of, 'My, what a nice-looking young man he is. And doesn't he just appear to adore Leah?''' She shifted her head so she could look at Leah. "And I remember thinking, 'Yeah, but how does Leah feel about him?'"

Leah averted her gaze, fussing with a fake rose Rachel had overlooked. The words sounded too similar to what J.T. has asked her that night in the supermarket parking lot. *Do you love him?*

"Dad liked him."

Rachel smiled. "Dad loved Dan." She gestured with her hand. "They had that whole legal thing in common. I think Dad looked upon Dan as his adopted son. One that would follow in his footsteps and one day become judge."

Leah smiled, remembering the relationship between her father and her husband. "I think that's what Dan wants, too."

Leah glanced at where her and her sister's feet swayed together then apart again on the coffee table.

"Are you having second thoughts about reconciling?" Rachel asked quietly.

Leah simply nodded, then bit hard on her bottom lip to keep from spilling the reason why.

"Then don't do it."

She squinted at her sister. It was the wine talking. It had to be the wine.

Rachel shifted until she was sitting up, her feet tucked underneath her. "I'm serious, Lee. If you're having second thoughts, don't you dare continue on with the reconciliation. It wouldn't be fair to Dan. And, more importantly, it wouldn't be fair to you.''

Leah swallowed hard as she put her feet on the floor and sat up straighter. "But Sami wants us to be a family again so much."

"And in three years Sami will want a car. Does that mean you're going to buy her one?"

Leah rolled her eyes.

"I'm serious, Lee. Before you know it Sami will be a teenager with a whole different slew of problems that have nothing to do with you and Dan. She'll be dating, planning her own future, thumbing through wedding magazines. And when that happens, where will you and Dan be? Heading for divorce court again?"

What her sister said made so much sense Leah didn't know how she hadn't seen it herself.

"Besides, silly, you guys are already a family. No, you may not live under the same roof, but you'll always be Sami's mother. And Dan will always be her father. And she'll always be your daughter and Dan's daughter." She shrugged as she put the bouquet back down. "I think it's time you admit that you're sick of being Miss Suzie Homemaker and start concentrating on a life of your own."

She reached for a box of something on the corner of the table. Leah realized it was chocolate. Rachel took her time picking one out for herself, then held it out to Leah who did the same. They both chewed on the candy thoughtfully.

"I have a life, you know."

Rachel smiled. "I know. You're going back to school. That's a good thing."

Leah shook her head as she chose another chocolate. "No. I'm not talking about just that."

And, surprisingly, she wasn't talking about J.T., either.

"Don't tell me you're hooking on the weekends down on Jefferson."

Leah threw her head back and laughed. "No worries there." She licked her fingers then reached for the wine glass with water in it. "I've been thinking about opening up a...lingerie shop."

Rachel was openly surprised. "What?"

Leah was a bit offended. "Don't act so shocked."

"Why not? That's exactly what I'm feeling right now." She grabbed the water bottle instead of the glass and nearly downed half the two liters of liquid. "I mean, come on, Leah. Over the past eleven years I haven't heard you talk about anything but Sami, the house and Dan."

Leah shrugged. "So?"

"So...so...opening a lingerie shop..." She suddenly bounced enthusiastically on the couch. "Oh, tell me about it! I mean, where did you get the idea? Where would you open it? What would you sell?"

Leah laughed, warming to the idea herself. She told her sister about meeting Ginger Wasserman five years ago when she'd set out to spice up her and Dan's lagging love life. The attempt to heat things up between the sheets had fizzled, but her friendship with Ginger had flourished. So much so that when Leah suggested Ginger expand, she hadn't hesitated to put her money where her mouth was and become a silent partner of the establishment.

And now Ginger was encouraging her to open a satellite shop in the West End. Something more up-scale and trendy, but with the same Women Only flavor.

"Oh, my god, I went to that place once," Rachel whispered, her eyes round. "Isn't that where they offer lessons in...in..."

"Massage therapy. Sexual acts. Belly dancing. You name it, WO offers it."

"I went there with Jenny. You remember Jenny— I went to high school with her. Anyway, part of her bachelorette party was a lesson in how to give a blow job that would blow his mind."

Leah smiled. "That would be the place." She cleared her throat and took the water from her sister, then drank some. "Although I don't think I'll be offering the same types of services in the West End."

"Oh, why not?" Rachel was excited. "It is for

'women only,' right? So it should cater to all of women's fantasies.''

And so ensued an hour-long discussion on Leah's possible plans. Plans that didn't include Dan or Sami or J.T. Plans that were strictly for her and her alone.

At some point during the conversation both of them had stretched out again, their feet on the coffee table, their heads touching as they stared at each other's toenail polish.

"You know what this means, don't you?" Rachel asked quietly.

Leah swallowed hard. "That Dan and Sami are going to hate it?'

Interestingly enough, she didn't think J.T. would. Not because she didn't know what he did or didn't like. She just had a feeling that he would support her in anything she wanted to do.

"Well, there is that.''

Leah lightly knocked her sister's foot.

"No, what this means is that you, big sister, are going to have give me one hell of a great wedding present." She laughed. "Well, that and a big discount.''

LATER THAT NIGHT, LEAH LAY in her gigantic bed, her arms crossed behind her head as she stared at the ceiling. For the first time in a very long time, she was smiling. Not because of something Sami did. Or J.T. Or even her sister. But because of something she was going to do.

She rubbed the bottom of her feet against the soft Egyptian cotton sheets and glanced at the clock. After eleven. Sami was already in bed asleep. Everything in the house that needed to be done was done. And she knew a nearly overwhelming urge to begin implementing her plans as soon as she could.

The telephone on the nightstand rang. She gave a start. Dan? It seemed likely. He was the only one who would call this late.

She picked up on the second ring.

"Leah?"

Definitely not Dan.

Her heart did a little flip in her chest and her palms instantly dampened. "J.T.?"

She heard what sounded like him moving the phone from one ear to the other then he cleared his voice. "Sorry to call so late. I hope I didn't wake you."

"No, no. I wasn't sleeping."

"I know. I can see your light on from here."

Leah sat up in bed and looked at the sheer-covered windows overlooking the street. She crossed the room and pulled back one of the gauzy curtains.

"To your left. Behind the van."

Leah made him out as he flicked his headlight on

and off. She felt ridiculously like a schoolgirl who would be caught by her father at any minute. "What are you doing out there?"

"I couldn't sleep, either," he said quietly.

"Give me a couple of minutes, I'll be right down."

"No. Don't," J.T. said. "That's not why I called."

Leah returned to the window, wishing she could make out his expression in the dark. "I don't understand...."

A soft chuckle then, "I called to ask you out for a date, Leah. You know, dinner. Maybe a movie."

Her stomach tightened. "What?" she whispered.

"Tomorrow night. Say at about seven?"

J.T. had driven to her house at eleven at night to ask her out on a date.

Leah was half afraid she had turned into that teenage girl sneaking around behind her parents' back.

Dan would be picking Sami up at around six tomorrow for the weekend. That would give her plenty of time to get ready to do whatever J.T. had in mind.

Of course she had been hoping to have that talk with Dan first....

"Leah, don't say no."

She smiled and turned her face from the window in case he could see her. "Yes," she said. "Yes,

J.T., I'd love to go out on a date with you tomorrow night.''

"Good. I'm glad to hear it.''

The line went silent as Leah got lost in her own thoughts. It had been a long time since she'd been out on a date. And the mere idea of going out on one with J.T. made her feel tingly all over.

She walked back to sit on her bed, running her hand over the soft bedding. "But that's tomorrow. What about tonight?''

His answering chuckle tickled her ear. "Tonight you need to get some rest, Leah. So shut off that light, get into bed and I'll pick you up at seven tomorrow night.''

Leah drew her hand from her neck down the front of her silky nightgown, almost feeling like J.T. could see her. Which was ridiculous. He couldn't see her through the sheers. "And you? What are you going to do tonight, Josh?''

She thought she heard him swallow hard. "I'm going to go back to the house and take a long, cold shower.'' A heartbeat of a pause, then, "Good night, Leah. Sweet dreams.''

Her grip tightened on the receiver. "Good night.''

As she hung up the phone she knew her dreams would be very sweet, indeed.

12

LEAH WAS EASILY THE MOST beautiful woman in the place. And J.T. was awed that he was the one she'd chosen to be with.

"This is nice," she said quietly, taking in the atmosphere of the upscale restaurant in downtown Toledo.

"You haven't been here before?" he asked.

"No. Well, yes, actually, I have. We…I used to come here a lot."

"With Dan."

She looked everywhere but at him. "Um, yes."

He'd made her uncomfortable. Damn. When he'd chosen the upscale restaurant, he hadn't considered that she might have been there with her ex-husband.

"We can go somewhere else," he suggested.

Her dark eyes widened. "No. I mean, unless you want to go somewhere else."

She had on a simple black dress that was anything but simple on her. It skimmed her trim figure, emphasizing the deep valley between her breasts, and the shapeliness of her legs as she crossed and re-crossed her legs at the elegant, linen-draped table.

"Oh, God," she said, her gaze catching on something just over his shoulder.

"Your ex?" he asked, his back stiffening.

"Worse. My sister."

LEAH WANTED TO SLINK UNDER the table and hide. Not because she was ashamed to be seen with J.T. Rather, she knew there was going to be hell to pay that she hadn't breathed word to her sister last night about J.T. being back in town.

She didn't delude herself into thinking Rachel wouldn't recognize J.T. During that summer so long ago her fourteen-year-old sister had been all gangly legs and doe eyes and had followed J.T. around like a puppy dog.

And Rachel was the only one who knew that J.T. was the man she'd had the affair with a year and a half ago.

"Look who's here, honey," Rachel said happily, none too discreetly trying to see the dark-haired man. "It's Leah and..."

She finally neared the table enough to see J.T.

"Oh, my God! Josh, is that you?"

Leah watched as J.T. rose to greet her sister, looking particularly yummy in the fitted dark suit he wore. Yes, she'd admitted when she'd joined him on the back of his bike, he cleaned up very well. It had been all she could do not to drag him into the house with her rather than go out on the date he had planned.

J.T.'s eyes were wary and amused as he considered her sister. "Rachel. It's been a while."

He took Rachel's hands in his and kissed her cheek, every bit the gentleman.

Leah finally found her legs and rose from the table as well, greeting first Gabe, then her sister.

"You little devil you," Rachel whispered into her ear under the pretense of kissing her cheek. "You are in so much trouble."

Leah's tight smile turned genuine. "You have no idea."

They turned to find Gabe and J.T. quietly discussing the NBA playoffs. Rachel took Leah's arm and leaned in. "Mmm. Delicious, aren't they?"

Leah had to admit they were. J.T. easily matched Gabe's six-foot-two height and was even wider across the chest and shoulders than her sister's fiancé. Both dark and mysterious, she guessed that neither would last a minute alone in a bar without some woman or other hitting on them.

One of the owners approached them. "Would you four like to dine together?"

Leah's gaze flew to J.T.'s face. This was their first date. She didn't want to spend it with her overcurious sister and her fiancé, no matter how much she loved them.

"Oh, let's!" Rachel's eyes sparkled in devilish delight, her motivations clearly selfish.

"Actually, Leah and I were just discussing that we're going to be late for our show." He took two tickets out of his inside jacket pocket, glanced at them, then put them back into his pocket. "Another time, maybe?"

Leah practically sighed with relief as her sister made a face at her. As they hugged goodbye, Rachel said for Leah's ears only, "You little minx. I expect details. Tonight. The instant you get home."

"Who's to say I'll be alone?" Leah whispered back, smiling at J.T. over her shoulder.

Rachel pretended shock, then reluctantly stood back to allow Leah to say goodbye to Gabe. Leah took J.T.'s arm, trying not to run from the restaurant.

"I know a great Italian place," Leah said, laughing as J.T. held the door open for her.

J.T. RELAXED INTO THE BURGUNDY leather booth, the environment of the Italian restaurant Leah had directed him to much more to his liking, although interestingly enough he was coming to feel comfortable with her wherever they were. There were no corny Italian murals on the walls, or plaster columns. Merely a warm atmosphere to enjoy a good meal and quiet conversation.

And he intended to do both tonight with the woman across from him.

He'd removed his suit jacket and loosened his tie, his shirtsleeves rolled up more to prevent spaghetti sauce from dropping onto them than a real need to be more casual.

Casual… Interesting that as dressed up as Leah was, she still looked at home in the family restaurant. Like she belonged. He hadn't expected that. But he realized he should have. Even when they were teens she'd fit right in with the other teens who'd stayed in tents and trailers rather than the mammoth cabins rimming the lake.

They enjoyed an oval medium pepperoni and mushroom pizza with thin, crispy crust and small plates of pasta, their wine in a carafe rather than a bottle. Leah reached to top off his glass and he took it from her, filling both their glasses himself.

She smiled and crossed her arms on top of the table. "So what's this about a show?" she asked.

J.T. grinned as he fished the two slips of paper from his jacket pocket hanging next to the booth. He handed them to her. Her laughter did something funny to his stomach.

"A comedy club?"

He nodded and glanced at his watch. "Do you want to go?"

She handed him the tickets back. "Do you?"

He shrugged as he put the tickets back into his jacket pocket. "I don't know. I'm having a good time where we are."

Her smile widened, making her look so much like that teenager he once knew she took his breath away. Although that self-confident teen wouldn't have asked what he thought, she would have just told him she didn't want to go. "Me, too."

She sat back and allowed the waitress to take her spaghetti plate away and provide a clean pizza plate. J.T. guessed the restaurant was used to lingering diners.

"You know," Leah said quietly. "I can't count the number of times you've told me you wanted to talk to me...."

J.T. took a long sip of wine, considering her over the rim.

"Now that you have my undivided attention—" she shrugged lightly "—shoot."

He didn't think for a minute she felt the nonchalance she pretended. The trembling of her fingers as she toyed with her napkin betrayed her underlying hesitation. He wasn't sure what she believed he wanted to discuss, but he did know that whatever it was scared her.

He silently bit off an oath for the man who had made Leah wary of life. Frightened to lay her emotions out on the table for all to see. Even as he admitted that man could be him.

He slowly shook his head. "The night is young. We can get around to that later."

She crossed her arms under her breasts, emphasizing the creamy half globes of delectable flesh visible in the deep V of black material. He'd have liked to run his tongue along that smooth flesh just then. Which made it a good thing that they were in a public place.

Leah smiled. "Then you won't mind if I ask you a few questions?"

"Shoot," he said, using her word.

She toyed with her wineglass, her expression growing more serious. J.T. couldn't help but tense. He knew what she was going to ask before she even asked it.

"What are you running from, J.T.?"

He pretended an interest in his callused hands, for a moment not recognizing them as his own.

Leah leaned slightly forward and lowered her voice, likely in case those around her could hear. "Every time you see a police car, you look like you're ready to bolt. Are you in some kind of trouble?"

J.T. cleared his throat, meeting her eyes dead on. "Yes, Leah, I am in trouble."

She blinked several times. Perhaps she had expected him to tell her it was her imagination. Come up with some kind of lame story to calm her fears. But that wasn't J.T.'s style. The truth was what he was good at, no matter how ugly.

"Can you share what kind of trouble you're in?"

Now answering that question was a little more difficult.

Her gaze skittered over his face and he wondered what his expression gave away. "It's that serious?"

"Serious enough to put a damper on the evening."

She glanced at her wineglass, her eyes growing dark and pensive. "But you will tell me? When you feel it's time?"

He nodded. "I will."

He only wondered how differently she would look at him when he did tell her.

LEAH'S SKIN TINGLED ALL OVER. She climbed from the back of the bike as carefully as she could, mindful of her dress, then looked in her purse for her keys. The house was dark and quiet, as was the neighborhood now that J.T. had turned off his bike. Her thighs still vibrated and she couldn't seem to ease the smile from her face, no matter the run in her nylon, the tangled state of her hair, or the spot of spaghetti sauce on the front of her dress.

Tonight she and J.T. had talked about nearly everything and anything under the sun. She'd shared amusing and somber details about her daughter, probably ad nauseam, while he'd told her of the places he'd been and the jobs he'd held. They'd reminisced about the summer they'd met and what they had thought of each other then, curiously avoiding talking about a year and a half ago and any mention of Dan and where her plans with him stood. He told her of the work he was doing now at the house outside of town and she told him of her wish to open another Women Only shop. As she'd guessed, he hadn't even lifted a brow. He'd merely grinned and said something about how he'd wondered where she'd gotten all that naughty underwear.

What had gone unsaid, however, was what trouble he was in and what he'd wanted to talk to her about, which she realized might be one and the same thing. The knowledge tied a small knot in her stomach, even though she knew J.T. could never do anything unforgivable. She felt it in her bone marrow.

It was well after midnight. They devoured the rest of the pizza, another carafe of wine and tiramisu for dessert, and then the restaurant manager practically had to boot them out so he could close up.

Now Leah's appetite had turned to more wicked things.

She walked up the sidewalk, overly aware of J.T.'s presence behind her.

She'd spent the better part of the morning rearranging her bedroom. For nearly twelve years it had remained the same. The furniture in the same position, the color scheme unchanged. But today she'd taken great relish in changing everything around and buying new bed linens. When she was done she'd barely recognized the room. And that was definitely a good thing. Especially considering that she planned to spend the rest of the night in it with J.T.

She unlocked the door and began to enter when he stayed her with a hand on her arm.

"This is where I say goodnight."

Leah blinked at him, incapable of registering his soft words. "Very funny."

His gentle grip on her arm increased. "I'm not trying to be funny, Leah. I'm trying to take this, whatever it is that exists between us, to another level."

She swallowed hard. He was serious.

"If I go inside with you, we both know I won't leave until morning." He cupped her chin and ran his thumb over her cheek and her bottom lip, turning her blood to warm honey.

"And the problem with that would be…?" she whispered, her heart skidding across her chest at his delicate touch.

He shook his head, his grin making her weak in the knees. "Do you have anywhere you need to be tomorrow?"

She didn't answer, still too surprised that he wasn't staying.

"Make a couple of sandwiches, grab a blanket and meet me out here at eleven in the morning. I want to take you for a ride."

Leah shivered, remembering the last time they'd taken a ride.

"Okay," she whispered. "But tonight…"

He leaned forward, trapping her words in her mouth with a gentle, hot kiss. "Good night, Leah."

Leah stood dumbstruck as he walked back to his bike, climbed on and rode away into the darkness. She didn't move for long minutes, trying to follow the breadcrumbs to figure out what J.T. was doing. It almost seemed like he was courting her.

Courting her.

She smiled faintly. That was a term her mother would have used.

She absently wrapped her arms around herself, it having been awhile since she'd thought of Patricia Dubois. Had it really been only about a year and a half since she'd died? What would she say about J.T. and her sketchy past with him?

She honestly couldn't say that she knew.

And what of J.T. courting her?

A small thrill ran over her skin, mixed with more than a touch of fear.

"Sometimes you just have to hold on for the ride, Leah," Patricia had once told her. "Because life sometimes doesn't let you sit in the driver's seat."

The problem was Leah wasn't sure if she was capable of holding on for the ride.

She turned and let herself into the large, empty house, the sound of glass crunching under her heels. She froze, realizing that the lights she'd left on had been shut off. She reached behind her and prevented the door from closing at the same time that she switched on the foyer light. The depression era glass vase that had sat on the side table holding daffodils was now scattered into pieces on the marble tile.

She strained her ears, listening for sounds inside the house as she fished her cell phone out of her purse and made her way back outside. J.T.'s line rang and rang. She disconnected and dialed another number. The 911 operator picked up immediately. "Please send the police. There's been a break-in."

13

J.T. STOOD IN THE SHADOWS of Leah's bedroom, listening as she saw the police officers out. When he'd left after kissing her at her door, he'd ridden a few blocks up then circled back, his body too revved up to return to the house to try to sleep just yet. He'd parked up the street and shut off his engine, wondering why the front door was ajar. He found out when two patrol cars approached from the opposite direction and pulled up in front of the house.

Not stopping to think they might be there for him, he'd climbed off his bike and rushed toward the officers, his heart hammering against his rib cage, a fear unlike any he'd known before clutching his stomach. Then he saw Leah standing on the front steps, holding her purse to her chest. An overwhelming sense of relief had flooded through him.

Then alarm had taken over. He'd come way too close to throwing himself in the path of the very people who threatened his freedom.

He'd melted into the shadows of her neighbor's hedge then backtracked to his Harley where he'd stayed, watching as the lights switched on in Leah's house, one by one, then were turned off again as the officers made a sweep of the place. As soon as they'd finished with the second floor, J.T. had circled around to the back and climbed up to the upstairs balcony and then let himself in through an open window. He'd closed it and locked it after himself and then stolen into Leah's bedroom, the scent of her flowery perfume filling his senses as he waited for the officers to leave. It sounded like they were doing that now.

He stepped to the window and watched through the sheers as the patrolmen conversed with each other on the street then got into their cars and drove away.

Minutes later Leah came into the room, backlit by the hall light, her blond hair a halo around her shadowy face.

"Don't turn on the light."

She gasped, her nerves apparently stretched to the limit as he watched her fight her desire to bolt.

J.T. stepped in front of her. She instantly leaned into him, her arms looking for comfort not passion. He held her tightly against him.

"Someone broke in," she whispered as he absorbed the worst of her shudder. "I can't tell if they took anything yet, but a few things were broken, drawers gone through."

J.T. looked around the room they stood in, aided by the hall light. "What about up here?"

Leah pulled back. Though she had probably walked through the house with the police officers, she must not have registered the tour. "It doesn't look like they made it up here. The police think maybe I interrupted them."

J.T. merely stood holding her for a long moment, thoughts playing along the fringes of his mind but his primary concern right then Leah's safety and his need to comfort her.

"Do you want to go back home with me tonight?" he asked, brushing her hair back from her face.

She gazed at him for what seemed like a long time. "I've never felt so scared to stay in my own house. I'm afraid if I leave I may not want to come back."

J.T. nodded, trying to ignore the heat rolling from her body and sliding over his.

"Stay with me?" she whispered.

He swore he could feel the beat of her heart against his chest. He slid his hands down her back, wondering if he dared remain with her in a place that she'd shared with her ex-husband.

She pressed her lips against his neck, her breath feathery and warm, her body soft and hot. "Please."

J.T. swept his hands up to her face, cupping her

head in his fingers. He searched her wide, fear-filled eyes knowing he could deny her nothing. It had taken everything he had to walk away from her earlier. Considering what had transpired since, he couldn't bring himself to leave this room, much less the house. Not when Leah needed him.

He lowered his mouth to hers, his intention a brief kiss. But when she melded against him, her breasts teasing him through the fabric of his shirt, her hips flush against his, he had neither the will nor the ability to pull away.

Her tongue curved into his mouth, exploring the recesses, offering up her own for discovery. J.T. moved his hands to her shoulders, holding her still as she began restlessly shifting against him, his want of her growing to uncomfortable proportions. He heard her low whimper as she spread her hands against his chest, then began unbuttoning his shirt. He stood completely still as she placed her wet mouth against his neck then slid down, kissing each inch of flesh she uncovered until she had undone his slacks and held his pulsing length in her palms.

The instant her mouth made contact with his erection, J.T. threw his head back and gritted his teeth against a groan. So sweet. So hot. She swirled her tongue around the knob of his arousal, wetting it, then lightly blowing before taking the tip into her mouth and applying suction.

Dear Lord, he was in danger of losing it right then and there.

She stroked her fingers down to the root of his erection, then dropped her right hand toward the crisp hair-covered sac, giving him a light squeeze that slightly slowed the flow of blood to his erection. Then she slid her mouth farther down his length, her tongue flicking against his sensitive skin, her lips closing so she might suck with each inch she took in. She wrapped her fingers around the base of his penis then began a slow, rhythmic stroke she followed with her mouth. Up and down, up and down. She hummed as if he was giving her this exquisite pleasure rather than the other way around.

J.T. threaded his fingers into her soft hair, torn between the desire to stop her and the need to press her even closer. It seemed as if every drop of blood in his body had rushed to his groin, feeding his arousal, robbing him of breath, of energy and his own will to move. Though she kept up the rhythm of her hand, she slid back her mouth to concentrate on the very tip, licking and sucking then licking again. He groaned at the sensation. When she moved to take in as much of him as she could, the world exploded into myriad reds and yellow behind his closed eyelids, his body shaking as he filled her mouth with proof of his desire for her.

Finally his muscles slowed their twitching, and

his breathing began to even out. J.T. cracked open his eyes to watch Leah lick every last drop of his semen from his erection.

He covered her fingers where she still held him, and slowly lifted her hands until she was forced to follow. He kissed her deeply, tasting himself on her tongue, drinking in everything that was her.

"Please," she whispered, dropping hungry kisses along the length of his jaw then back to his mouth. "Make love to me, Josh."

Make love to her. Not have sex with her. Not screw her until she couldn't see straight.

No, she'd asked him to make love to her.

J.T.'s heart pounded unsteadily in his chest as he gazed down into her beautiful, shadowy face. His fingers found the V of her dress, then followed the fabric down over her full breasts, briefly cupping them before reaching behind to tug down her zipper. The sound of the metal teeth in the silence of the room was erotically enticing. He edged the fabric down over her shoulders, giving it a slow shove until it pooled around her ankles and she stepped out of it. Underneath she had on the most decadent of lacy black bras and a garter belt that held up her dusky nylons. Noticeably missing was any sign of panties.

He groaned and swept her up into his arms, carrying her to the bed a couple of feet away. The sweet scent of gardenias filled his senses as he laid her against the dozen or so pillows. Then he hovered above her to take his visual fill of her.

Her creamy skin emerged even paler against the black of her undergarments, her breasts heaving as she took a deep, ragged breath. Her waist was narrow and slender and trembling under his visual onslaught. Her thighs rested together but he knew it would only take one touch and she would open to him fully, inviting him in.

J.T. knew there had to be a time when he didn't want this woman, but damned if he could remember when. From the moment he'd first met her she'd crawled under his skin and stolen in his heart. It had been love at first sight, although he hadn't known it at the time. He had been too young to recognize the emotion for what it was. He'd assumed himself that it was strictly lust and that it would pass. But it never had. With every touch, every kiss, his want of her grew and grew until he accepted that she was the only one who could soothe the thunderous desire that roared through him.

And he knew with everything that he was that she felt the same even though she might not be near admitting it.

He gazed into her eyes at the same time he guided his hand to brush against the quivering flesh of her stomach. She caught her breath and swallowed hard, as she fought to hold his gaze. He trailed his fingers down lower until they rested against her springy blonde curls, then he tunneled into them, parting her slick folds so he might tease the tight bud hiding there.

Leah's eyes drifted closed and she moaned, her hips involuntarily coming up off the mattress. Her glorious lips were parted and her breath came in ever quickening gasps. He trailed his fingers farther south, into her dripping channel, then slid two inside her silken heat, all the time watching her cheeks flush, her chest heave, her movements grow more and more restless.

The realization that he hadn't brought protection hit him like a bright light in the eyes. He had purposely left his condoms in his duffel back at the house so he wouldn't be tempted to give in to his physical need for her.

To ask her for it now…

He'd known when they'd first come together on the back of his bike that she hadn't been with anyone for a long, long time. Had felt it in her tightness, in her quick race to orgasm. And aside from a single quick, faceless, protected encounter, he hadn't been with anyone else since leaving her.

His body quaked at the prospect of feeling Leah's unadulterated heat surrounding him. Feeling her slick need for him without latex separating them. Her muscles convulsing around his. Allowing his juices to mix with hers. Recognizing the possibility that their union could create another human life.

Her soft moans told him she was nearing crisis stage. He slowly withdrew his fingers, ignoring her sound of protest. He spread her thighs open to him then positioned himself there. She blinked her eyes open, he'd like to think because she felt the desire for a visual connection with him as much as he did.

"I have no protection, Leah," he murmured, bending down to kiss the smooth ridge of her collarbone. "I want to make love to you without it."

She swallowed hard, her expression unchanged. Then she nodded slowly. "Yes."

The meaning behind that one word sent a foreign sensation skimming through J.T.'s veins along with his intense desire for her. He thought it might have been joy. A happiness, a contentment so profound, that for a moment he wasn't able to move.

He felt Leah's hand on his pulsing erection, her gaze holding his as she purposefully guided him to her.

J.T.'s entire body shook as he breached her unprotected entrance. Her body hotly welcomed him, her juices like warmed honey pouring over his rigid flesh, her muscles drawing him in. The scent that reached his nose, their scent, not his, not hers, but theirs, without the tinge of latex, further amplified his heightened state. He slowly slid in to the hilt, watching as her eyes briefly fluttered closed.

The climax that followed rolled through him like distant and rumbling thunder. Leah clung to him, her deep gasp and intense contractions speaking of her own intense reaction.

Although he'd known it with his heart, the power rocked him now to his soul. He loved this woman. Always had. Always would.

LEAH HAD NEVER KNOWN a pleasure so complete, so earth-shattering, as she sat under the shade of the oak on the property where J.T. worked, her shorter limbs tangled with his longer ones. Her back flush against his front, his arms holding her firmly to his chest.

It seemed they hadn't been more than a few inches apart since last night, rising late this morning to take a long ride on his bike, then ending up back here where they'd leisurely fed each other the light picnic she'd packed.

"I hope none of your neighbors get curious and come up the drive," she murmured, rubbing her nose against the side of his neck.

He smiled into her hair. "My neighbors never get that curious."

She knew a moment of sadness. "That must be difficult. Always being alone."

J.T.'s hand stilled on her bare back. "You get used to it."

She shivered, caused by both the touch of his hand and the coolness of the spring breeze. "I don't think I could ever get used to that."

Long moments passed where neither of them said anything. Leah listened to the fresh blooms on the tree rustle, the chirp of a cardinal jumping from branch to branch above them.

"I love you, you know that, don't you?" he murmured, kissing her temple and gathering her close.

Leah burrowed her face against his arm, feeling as if her smile began somewhere in the vicinity of her heart.

"Sometimes I think I was born loving you. I just didn't know it until I met you."

Her smile widened, his words giving her heart wings. "I love you, too," she whispered, surprised to hear the proclamation exit her lips.

His hold on her tightened.

"I needed to hear that, Leah." He kissed her shoulder. "You have no idea how much I needed to hear that."

She snuggled her bottom against him, feeling him rise to the occasion.

"And I hope that what I have to say doesn't change that."

J.T.'s HEART POUNDED, so full of joy, so full of grief, as he lay with Leah on the red and black wool blanket she had brought with them.

He wasn't sure when he had decided to tell her. He only knew an incredible need to purge himself of the secret he'd kept locked inside for far, far too long.

"I'm wanted for murder, Leah."

He tensed, waiting for her to stiffen, pull away, show some sign that she was not only shocked by the news but repulsed. Her fingers stilled where she had been running them up and down his arm, but he sensed no other physical reaction to his words.

"But you didn't do it."

A statement, not a question.

He knew a relief so profound he was dizzy with it. "No."

She didn't move for long moments, then she turned in his arms to face him, her eyes full of pain. For him. "Tell me."

J.T. swallowed hard. He'd never shared the secret with anyone, not even his father, although the old man had found out through the local authorities when they'd come knocking on his door.

"Her name was Felicia Dumont and she was married to someone else...."

He haltingly told her of a woman he'd known over a decade ago in a small town outside Phoenix,

Arizona. A woman who had been closer to his age than her husband's. A woman who had seduced him with her sadness and her body. A woman who had been the complete opposite of Leah. Which was what he'd thought he needed to help exorcise Leah's ghost when he'd discovered she'd gotten married.

A woman who had been killed in the motel room bed where they'd just had sex. A woman whose murder had been pinned on him.

Leah had remained quiet through his confession, making no comment, showing no emotion other than understanding.

"The evidence was convincing. My semen had been found on her body. The room had been in my name." He swallowed hard, remembering returning to the motel room to find the place swarming with cops. He'd ducked into the shadows and had been hiding in them ever since. "I avoided arrest and contacted an attorney who was negotiating the terms of my surrender. But despite his contacts with the nearby Phoenix P.D., Felicia's husband had more. You see, he was the sheriff of the county where the murder occurred, and also the son of a wealthy ranch owner. Through friends and contacts my attorney uncovered how extensive the evidence against me was and told me that turning myself over would be like walking straight to the execution chamber."

Leah's hair blew in the light breeze. "So you ran."

He met her gaze. "So I ran."

She laid her head against his chest and squeezed him so hard that for a moment he couldn't breathe. "What it must have been like for you all these years," she whispered. "Always having to hide. To run."

J.T. closed his eyes, wishing he never had to let her go. She didn't ask him the details of the gruesome murder. Didn't request information about his plans. She was concerned about how life had been for him in the years since.

He smoothed her hair down then placed a lingering kiss to the top of her head. "I've decided now's the time I stop running."

14

LEAH TRIED TO ABSORB the importance of what he was telling her, but couldn't move beyond the panic accumulating in her stomach. "What did you just say?"

He lifted her chin so that he could gaze into her face, then smiled sadly at her. "I said it's time for me to stop running, Leah."

"But…why? Why now?"

"Because I now know something that's more important than my freedom, Leah. I now know you love me."

Emotion sure and swift crowded her chest, making it difficult to breathe, impossible to talk. "But…" she said, his handsome face becoming a blur through the tears that burned her eyes.

"Shh. I know who did it, Leah. I just have to find a way to prove it."

"What if you can't prove it? Oh, Josh, I can't lose you now. Not now that I've found you again."

He sat up and gathered her into his arms, draping his denim shirt over her naked body to shield her from any possible curious eyes and the cool breeze. "I'll be done with the house on Monday, Leah. What do I do next? I can't rent a place—"

"I'll rent one for you."

"I can't get a job that requires my social security number—"

"You'll keep doing what you're doing."

He smiled at her sadly. "And what are you going to do? Hide with me whenever a police car passes? And what if they catch whiff of my trail and find me here in Toledo? Do I run? Do you run with me?"

It all loomed so impossibly dark and difficult.

"No," he said quietly. "I'll find a way to make this work."

"And what if you can't? What if they catch up with you before you can prove your innocence?"

He ran a finger down the length of her cheek, making her realize her skin was damp with tears. "Then you'll help me, won't you, Leah?"

She held him so tightly she cut off the circulation of blood to her arms. "Yes. Yes, I'll help you."

She prayed it wouldn't come to that.

TWO DAYS LATER LEAH FOUGHT to concentrate on her notes, her gaze constantly drawn to the kitchen clock. All her life she'd been surrounded by the law.

First as the daughter of a judge. Then as the wife of a prominent defense attorney.

It seemed ironic, then, that she was in love with someone who was on the other side of it.

"Phoenix," she scribbled down. "Felicia Dumont. Husband?"

Ever since J.T. had shared his secret with her, it seemed as if it now hovered over both of them. Their lovemaking had become more somber, more serious, more intense. And one of the most difficult things she'd ever done was come home last night to meet Sami when Dan brought her back from their weekend together. After her daughter had gone to bed, she and J.T. had spent hours on the phone, sometimes saying nothing, other times everything.

Then, this morning he'd set out to finish up the last of his work on the house, she'd gone to class, and now just after noon, she was sitting at the kitchen island making notes to herself.

J.T. was convinced that Felicia's husband was behind the murder of his wife. He figured the older man had discovered his young wife was having an affair and determined to end it one way or another. Only J.T. had no idea it would be by killing Felicia and framing him for her murder.

But how did you prove that in the face of such overwhelming evidence against J.T.?

On a fresh page, she wrote down names of possible defense lawyers in the area she might consult with, tapping the pencil against the pad when she realized that they were all friends or associates of Dan. She tore the sheet off and balled it up, smoothing the side of her hand against the paper as she tried to think of what else she might be able to do.

The name of the attorney in Phoenix. J.T. hadn't told her it. She wrote that down.

She picked up the pad to go up to Sami's room. Her daughter wasn't due home from school for another two hours, certainly enough time to do some Internet surfing on the girl's computer without her even knowing it.

The phone rang as she was passing. She clutched the pad to her chest and picked up the extension.

"Leah? Oh, God, Leah, Dad's in the hospital," her sister's voice filled her ear. "He's had a heart attack."

LEAH PACED THE FLOOR OUTSIDE of St. Vincent Mercy Medical Center's emergency ward, Rachel sitting nearby with her arms crossed and her skin paler than Leah had ever seen it. Over an hour had passed since her sister had called her and they still hadn't heard anything on their father's condition. All they knew was that he'd been driving back from Columbus and had been life-flighted to the hospital just after noon.

"Why won't someone tell us what's happening?" she murmured, walking over to the nurses' station for the third time in fifteen minutes and asking for an update. The round, black nurse behind the safety glass shook her head and told her she'd let them know as soon as she heard anything, saying the same thing she had on the prior occasions Leah and Rachel had asked.

There was a secondary waiting area just off the side of the main lobby where they could have sat, out of the way of the other patients waiting for medical attention, but neither Rachel nor Leah wanted to be away from where they might hear word.

Leah watched as an older man clutching his left arm was walked through the automatic sliding glass doors by a young woman. An orderly hurried forward with a wheelchair then pushed him through the nearby double-hinged doors.

"God, I always thought he was indestructible, you know?" Rachel whispered, her gaze on the same man who had just disappeared. She covered her face with her hands. "I knew I should have been making him eat healthier foods for Sunday brunch. All that oil and butter and cream…"

Leah took the seat next to her and pulled Rachel's hand into her lap. "Sunday brunch is not to blame for this," she said with an attempt at a smile.

"We've both been trying to talk Dad into getting a physical."

She felt Rachel's shudder. "He spent so much time in the hospital, so much time around doctors while Mom was dying, he said that he'd had his fill of both for some time to come."

The sisters fell silent. Leah thought about all the family had gone through a year and a half ago with the death of their mother from breast cancer. Of course, they'd had time to prepare then. Had watched as Patricia Dubois had grown thinner and thinner, her cancer unresponsive to any treatment as it slowly ate away at her insides.

It wasn't fair that they should be at risk of losing their father so soon after losing their mother. But Leah had long ago come to understand that very little about life was fair.

Jonathon Dubois was only a shade over fifty-five. Certainly not anywhere near what any of them considered old. But even Leah knew that age had very little to do with heart disease.

A resident wearing green scrubs came through the swinging doors to the emergency room. Leah and Rachel both got to their feet, Leah's knees almost refusing to hold her weight.

"Ms. Dubois?" he said, looking for Rachel, who had been the first of them to arrive.

"How is he?" Rachel said.

"We've stabilized him and he's resting calmly right now."

Leah was dizzy with relief. "Thank God. Where is he? Can we see him?"

The young doctor shook his head. "No, I'm sorry. The angiography shows that he's suffering from major blockages in three arteries. We've scheduled him for immediate coronary artery bypass surgery."

Rachel sank back to her chair, her hazel eyes wide and unseeing.

"Five minutes," Leah begged, searching the man's eyes. "Just five minutes. That's all we ask."

He looked at her long and hard, then sighed and glanced at his watch. "Okay. Five minutes."

The two sisters followed the resident in through the swinging doors. Leah tried not to look at the curtained off cubicles on either side of her, filled with patients with varying illnesses, but failed. In one a tube was being fed down a young boy's throat. In another, a woman lay on an examining table crying and clutching her stomach.

At the end of the hall the resident stopped and pointed to the right. Leah went inside and immediately stopped in her tracks.

If she hadn't been told that the ashen, gray-haired man lying against the sheets was her father, she might never have recognized him. It seemed as if all the color had been drained from his skin, robbing it of elasticity and tone. A breathing tube and oxygen mask were attached as were heart monitors and a slew of machines she couldn't begin to identity.

In that one moment Judge Jonathon Dubois looked thirty years older than his age.

Rachel went to his side first and his eyes drifted open. Leah looked toward the resident who was making a notation on the chart.

"The attack took a lot out of him and we've given him medication," he explained.

She swallowed hard and stepped up next to her sister who was softly scolding him.

"I've been after you and after you to start eating healthier," she was saying, tears bright in her eyes, though a smile softened her words. "But no, you always had to go for that extra serving of hollandaise sauce."

Jonathon smiled and tried to remove the oxygen mask.

"No, leave it on, Daddy," Leah said. "We can hear you."

"I wanted to say that you sound just like your mother, Rachel."

"They're going to operate on you. You understand that, don't you?" Leah asked.

His eyes twinkled at her. "I just had a heart attack, I didn't go stupid, Lee. I'm still in full control of my mental faculties."

She suppressed a watery laugh.

"I'm sorry," the resident said, appearing in the hall outside the curtained off area. "I'm going to have to ask that you leave now."

Leah leaned forward and kissed her father's cheek, wondering at how cold his skin was. Rachel did the same, swiping at the lipstick they'd both left behind.

"We'll see you soon, Daddy," Leah said quietly, hoping that was the case.

The resident left them to find their own way out. Leah watched over her shoulder as her father's bed was wheeled out and taken in the opposite direction.

"Oh, God, *Sami,*" she whispered, looking at her watch as Rachel led the way back out into the lobby. "I forgot about Sami."

FOR THE FIRST TIME IN A LONG TIME J.T. wished he had a car instead of a motorcycle. He parked the Harley across the street from Ottawa Hills Elementary School, watching as children in green, blue and white uniforms filed out of the three-story brick building. When Leah had called him fifteen minutes ago saying her father had been rushed to the hospital, and that she hadn't been able to get in touch with her ex-husband, he'd instantly agreed to pick up her eleven-year-old daughter from school and bring her to the hospital.

He'd washed up as best he could, given the limited time he'd had, and changed his T-shirt, but his jeans bore smears of wood stain and his fingernails looked like he'd spent an hour digging through the dirt.

He pushed his longish hair from his face and scanned the cookie-cutter kids, looking for the little girl with the light brown hair he'd only seen up close once.

There. There she was. She was walking from the double doors with her backpack slung over her shoulder talking to two other girls flanking her. He didn't think waving to her would be such a good idea so he headed in her direction, determining to meet her halfway up the school walk.

"Hello, Sami," he said, smiling at her and the two girls she was with.

She squinted up at him against the sun, her eyes wary.

One of her friends elbowed her. "Who's that?" she asked in a disapproving tone.

"He's the plumber," Sami said with disdain.

"I'm J. T. West," he said, extending his hand to her. "Nice to make your acquaintance."

The two little girls shook his hand and told them their names were Courtney and Heather. Then they giggled and hurried away.

"What are you doing here?" Sami asked stonily, clutching her backpack more tightly.

"Your grandfather's taken ill, Sami. Your mom asked if I would drive you to the hospital."

He narrowed his eyes, watching as the eleven-year-old started backing away from him. "You're lying."

He tried to keep his face neutral. "I wish I were, Sami."

Her gaze passed him to the bike parked on the street.

"You're going to take me on that?"

J.T. gave in to the threatening grimace. "That's all I have."

He noticed the way the other students and their parents were beginning to look at them and knew an urgency to get out of there as quickly as possible.

"Look, call your mom if you want," he said, holding out his cell phone.

Sami started shaking her head and backing away more quickly toward the school building. "I don't believe you."

She turned and started running toward the building. J.T. easily caught up and grasped her schoolbag, knowing it was a mistake the instant his fingers touched Leah's daughter.

"Help! Help! He's trying to kidnap me!"

15

LEAH KNEW A FEAR so encompassing she was surprised she could still function.

Her hand shook as she held her cell phone to her ear, standing in the middle of the emergency waiting room with no concept of time or space. "What?" The word exited her mouth as little more than a whisper.

Her ex-husband's voice traveled over the airwaves, strong and determined. "I said someone tried to kidnap our daughter. Where are you?"

Leah didn't so much sit in the hard plastic chair as she did collapse into it. "Where is she?"

Rachel stared at her. "What is it, Leah? What's wrong?"

She ignored her sister who had sat down next to her, clutching her arm.

Dan said, "Sami's in the car with me now. We've just left the school. Where are you?"

"I'm at the hospital," she told him, then briefly outlined her father's situation, her mind swimming with everything that had transpired that day. "What happened with Sami? Who tried to kidnap her? Where?''

Dan sighed heavily into her ear as if he couldn't be bothered with the details. ''Suffice it to say they caught the guy.''

''Where?'' Leah demanded, dread coating her insides like so much tar.

It couldn't be…Sami wouldn't accuse…

''Outside the school,'' Dan said.

It could and Sami had.

Leah leaned forward, afraid she was going to hyperventilate. ''Let me talk to her.''

There was a pause, then Dan said, ''She's not up to talking right now, Lee. She's pretty shaken up.''

''Put her on the phone,'' Leah stood firm.

Long moments later she head Sami's voice. ''Mom?''

''What happened?''

Leah was half afraid the connection had cut off or that her daughter had handed the phone back to her father. ''That plumber guy tried to kidnap me.''

Oh God, oh God, oh God…

Leah rocked back and forth in the unaccommodating chair. This wasn't happening. It wasn't possible this was happening.

''I was really scared, Mom. I mean—''

''Hand the phone back to your father,'' she whispered.

"But Mom—"

"Just do as I say, Sami."

A moment later Dan's irritated voice sounded in her ear.

She asked, "Where have they taken him?"

A pause.

"Where?" she nearly shouted again.

"What are you talking about? To jail, I suspect. But what's—"

"Find out where and meet me there," she told him. "It shouldn't be too difficult for you since most of your clients come from there."

"What's the matter with you, Leah? I've never heard you—"

"Just do it!"

She pressed the disconnect button, her hand shaking so violently she nearly dropped the phone.

"Leah? Damn it, tell me what's going on," Rachel demanded, grasping her arm tightly.

"J.T.'s been arrested."

J.T. ACCEPTED IT AS A GIVEN. Women were destined to be his downfall.

He closed his eyes, visually blocking out the holding cell surrounding him, as he ticked off in his head the women he'd known. There was the woman who had made him fall in love with her during that perfect summer so long ago. The woman who had

drawn him into her sad web and whose death had
stamped him with the label murderer. Now there
was the woman—the girl—who'd pinned him for a
crime he hadn't committed because she was upset
with her mother and the world in general.

J.T. leaned against the wall in the corner of the
holding cell. He had his legs crossed at the ankles
and his hands in his pockets, but the relaxed stance
was deceptive because his blood pumped through
his body in triple time.

One minute he'd been doing Leah a favor by
picking up her daughter. The next he was being re-
strained by school security guards, then passed on
to police officers to be booked and shoved into a
jail cell.

Kidnapping. He'd been arrested for attempted
kidnapping.

He tugged his right hand out of his pocket and
rubbed the back of his neck, recalling Sami's tearful
face and her screams for someone to help her when
he'd reached for her to stop her from running away
from him. His first concern had been for her. It had
ripped his heart out to see her so upset and know
that he was the cause of it, however unjustified.

But when the guards had subdued him and J.T.
had calmly asked Sami to verify his story that he
was a friend of her mother, the eleven-year-old had
lifted her chin defiantly and told the officers that he

was a complete stranger and that he had tried to kidnap her.

J.T.'s mind went numb at the idea.

Now it was only a matter of time before the Ottawa Hills Police Department matched one J. T. West, attempted kidnapper, with Joshua Thomas Westwood, wanted murderer.

On a seat nearby, some poor Joe slept off his drug of choice, an occasional snore that sounded remarkably like a death rattle punctuating the overall silence of the room.

J.T. found it ironic that he'd been talking about turning himself in just two days ago. Finally facing what he'd been running from for so long. Wanting to work toward proving his innocence.

Somehow he'd never seen everything going down like this.

Leah…

His stomach clenched at the thought of her reaction when she heard the news. First she had her father's health scare to contend with. Now she had to face that her daughter was responsible for putting him behind bars…perhaps for life. He grimaced. If he was lucky. If he wasn't faced with execution by lethal injection when they transferred him back to Arizona.

The wild card in the entire situation was how quickly he would be sprung. The longer he stayed penned up, the more likely it became that the police would link him to his past.

LEAH WASN'T HAVING MUCH LUCK with the desk sergeant at the police station. Somewhere in the back of her mind she knew it didn't help that she looked like hell and that her movements were frantic, her demeanor panicky. All she could think about was that somewhere in the low building J.T. was locked up and she was responsible for it, no matter how indirectly.

"You've got to listen to me," she pleaded, her hands white where she had them pressed against the desk. "J. T. West is innocent. My daughter made a mistake." Her words were falling on deaf ears. "If you don't believe me, call the school principal. I contacted her ahead of time to inform the school I was having a friend pick up my daughter—"

"Leah?"

She swung around to face her ex-husband. She instantly relaxed even though his stony expression sent uneasiness swimming through her bloodstream. "Oh, thank God, you're here." She looked around him to where Sami was trying her best to look invisible.

Leah grabbed her daughter by the shoulder and brought her to stand in front of her. "What were you thinking?"

Dan placed his hands on Sami's slender shoulders. "No, Leah, I think the question here is what were you thinking?"

Leah slowly rose, meeting her ex-husband's steady gaze. "Excuse me?"

A muscle ticked in Dan's jaw. "You sent a complete stranger to pick up our daughter. What would you have her think?"

So Sami had told her father the truth. At least she wasn't sticking to her kidnapper story. But that didn't make the current situation any more bearable. J.T. was sitting in a jail cell, his very life on the line.

She looked into her ex-husband's irate face, anger beginning to replace her former panic. "J. T. West is not a stranger. Not to me, not to our daughter. And Sami's well aware of that."

Dan blinked at her, then looked at their daughter. "Is that true, Sami?"

For a moment Leah was afraid her daughter would play dumb. That she would claim she'd been momentarily confused, hadn't immediately recognized him, something to make the situation easier on her. Then her face fell and she dropped her gaze. "He's the man I told you about, Daddy. The one who came over and fixed our washing machine."

Leah stared at her husband hopefully, watching

as disappointment flickered over his features. "Now, can you please do something about getting J.T. out of here?" she asked.

"WEST!"

J.T. squinted at the officer unlocking the cell door with a clank of metal against metal.

"Charges have been dropped. You're free to go."

Free to go...

The words emerged so far from the ones he had expected to hear that for a moment he couldn't move. Then he was striding toward the door with purpose. The sooner he was out of the station the better. He didn't know why they hadn't discovered his secret, but he wasn't waiting around to find out.

LEAH WAS LONG PAST READY to jump out of her skin, her legs beginning to ache from all the pacing she'd done in the past few hours. Dan had explained the situation to the desk sergeant, who unsurprisingly knew Dan's name, and then another officer was called to release J.T.

She caught sight of her daughter who was sitting on a chair set against the far wall. The bow that had held her light brown hair had come loose and strands hung in front of her sulky face.

Leah took her thumbnail out from between her teeth and moved to stand in front of Dan. "I want you to take Sami home with you tonight."

Her daughter's gaze flew to her, but Leah refused to meet it, incapable of civilly addressing her daughter in that one moment.

"Can't do it, Lee," Dan said, his expression having returned to stony after arranging to have J.T. released. Apparently he was waiting around to see this "friend" of hers that their daughter disliked so much. "I'm neck deep in this murder case right now. It was all I could do to get the judge to call a recess until tomorrow morning so I could pick up Sami at the school."

"I don't care what you have going on, Dan. I don't think it's a good idea for Sami to be anywhere near me right now. Rearrange your schedule. Take her to your parents. I don't care. Just be a goddamn parent for once instead of relying on me to take up the slack."

He blinked at her, wariness in his eyes.

Leah was distantly aware of how cold her words sounded, but she couldn't help herself. She could take her daughter's indifference and all around bad behavior when it was directed toward her, but what she had done to J.T....

She shuddered as she thought of the chain of events Sami could have set off with her little stunt.

She would deal with her daughter tomorrow, when she had a clearer head. Right now she needed to focus on J.T. To see if there was some way to undo the damage that had been done.

Dan gave Leah one last look then glanced at their daughter. "Let's go, Sami."

The girl slowly got up and took her father's hand, both of them staring at Leah as if she were the enemy.

"You and me," she said to her daughter, "we're going to have a long talk when you get home. And need I say that it's not going to be pretty?"

Sami didn't reveal if she'd heard her one way or the other as Dan turned and they walked toward the door.

There was movement behind her. Leah turned to find J.T. striding toward her looking better than any man had a right to.

Her stomach bottomed out as she flung herself into his arms, holding him tight.

"Let's get out of here," he said evenly, his hands fiercely holding her to his side.

HE WAS LEAVING HER AGAIN....

Leah knew J.T. was right. It was only a matter of time before the authorities came knocking at her door looking for him.

But she couldn't bear the thought of being without him. And as irrational as the emotion was, she couldn't help feeling that he was leaving her all over again.

Dusk was settling over the impossibly flat farmland surrounding them, the empty two-lane road seeming to point like an arrow away from her. After picking him up at the station, she'd taken him to retrieve his bike, then together they had gone to the house where he had just finished up his work so he could collect his duffel and sleeping bags. It chilled Leah to the core to know that this was how he'd lived his life for the past ten years. That all he had to his name could be strapped to the back of his bike.

He had followed her home and together they had ridden to the same spot where they had made love that first time since he'd come back into her life. She wasn't wearing his leather coat this time, but her own windbreaker. And the spring air seemed to chill her to the bone where she sat on the bike next to where he stood.

"Where will you go?" she whispered, breathing in his profile as he considered the road to the west.

He slowly moved his gaze to her face. "Phoenix."

She shuddered and shoved her hands deeper into her pockets. What ifs piled up in her mind like unwanted pages from a newspaper. What if the authorities were waiting for him to come back and arrested him on sight? What if he wasn't able to prove his innocence? What if the true killer caught up with him first and got rid of him, too?

She shuddered so violently she nearly slipped from the bike.

J.T.'s fingers cupped her chin. She tried to fight him as he lifted her face to look into his.

"Take me with you," she whispered fervently.

She thought of her father in the hospital—she'd called Rachel to find out that he'd come through surgery okay and was now in Recovery. She thought of her daughter who, it appeared, would stop at nothing to prevent Leah from moving on with her life. She thought of her business plans and her sister and her house.

And knew in that one moment that she would give it all up to be by J.T.'s side.

He gave her a smile, one full of grief and sadness and admiration. "I can't do that, Leah."

Her chest tightened with emotion. "Yes, you can. Just let me stop by the house and pack a few things. I have money, too. We can just ride off into the sunset and never look back."

"And Sami?" he murmured.

Leah gazed at the smears of red and purple on the horizon. "Her father can look after her."

He turned her face back to his. "Could you really

live without knowing how your daughter was doing? Without being a part of her life?''

The swirling emotions in her stomach balled up into her throat on a sob. No, she couldn't. No matter what her daughter had done, how awful she had been, she couldn't just leave her behind.

''I want you to promise me that you'll follow up with the police on that break-in,'' J.T. said quietly. ''If anything happens out of the ordinary, call 911 immediately.''

She stared at him, unable to compute that he was worried about her when he had so much to be worried about for himself.

''I'll be back, Leah,'' he said quietly.

She wildly searched his face, wanting so badly to believe him but afraid to.

He bent to kiss her, his mouth hot and gentle and so full of love the tears burning the back of her eyelids ran down her cheeks unchecked.

''How can I believe that?'' she whispered. ''If you're not able to clear your name, how do I know you won't stay away in some outdated chivalrous manner to protect me? What if you go to prison? How will I know?''

He leaned his forehead against hers. ''I'll write asking you to send me cookies.''

Her stomach lurched. ''And to tell me to stay away?''

He abruptly moved away from her, stepping toward the west, his silhouette strong and powerful against the dimming light.

"What if the real killer kills you?" she whispered.

They both knew that the questions she posed were all very real possibilities.

"What would you have me do?" J.T. said evenly. He slowly turned to face her. "Tell me, Leah. What do you think I should do?"

She wanted to shout for him to stay there, in Toledo. But even as she thought it, she knew it was an impossibility. As a result of his arrest tonight, the time clock J.T. was racing against had begun ticking even faster. It was no longer safe for him there.

It was no longer safe for him anywhere.

Leah was so torn she wanted to cry out from the pain of it all. She wanted to tell him to ride to Alaska. Canada. Anywhere away from possible harm or arrest. But to do that would also take him away from her.

She blinked up through her tears to find J.T. standing in front of her, a dark, handsome man who had not only touched her soul, but had stolen it from her.

She searched his face. "My father's a judge. My sister's an attorney. I'm going to do everything in my power to see what they can do to help." She wrote their names and numbers on a piece of paper she took from her purse then pressed it into his hand. "If you can't call me, call them if you run into trouble. They'll help you."

He smiled at her sadly. "Trust me, Leah."

She caught her bottom lip between her teeth and bit down hard then nodded.

She only wished it was only him that she had to trust. Sadly, she was afraid it was herself, and her own traitorous emotions, that would ultimately betray her. And create a living hell from which she'd never be free.

He was leaving her again....

16

LEAH SPENT A RESTLESS NIGHT at home longing for J.T. with every fiber of her being and fearing he was gone forever. She'd also imagined every creak and every shadow was her unknown intruder. Now, early the next morning, she stood outside her father's private room, unable to bring herself to look inside. She heard Rachel's soft voice as she spoke, but couldn't make out her words.

She felt so far outside everything that felt familiar and comforting to her. J.T. was gone. The house had felt achingly empty without Sami there. And her father was lying in a hospital bed in the next room having come closer to death than she cared to consider.

The doctor had requested that she and her sister take turns during visitations so as not to overwhelm their father so soon after surgery. Since Rachel had spent most of the day yesterday in the waiting room, Leah had told her to go first. She glanced at where Rachel's fiancé, Gabe, stood down at the end of the hall, tall, dark and incredibly handsome even given his present environs. He'd come to the hospital even though he'd known he wouldn't be able to see Jonathon. He'd flown back from California late last night to support and be there for the woman he loved.

The knowledge made her heart ache even more acutely.

Rachel came out of the room, pausing for a moment next to Leah. Animation had returned to her face, but her eyes still looked haunted.

"How is he?" Leah asked.

"Ornery as ever." Rachel pushed her short dark hair back from her face. "But why don't you be the judge of the judge? He's waiting for you."

Rachel gave her a hug, pausing for a moment as if wanting to ask her something. Instead she walked down the hall and melted into Gabe's arms.

Leah briefly closed her eyes, steeling herself for what she was about to see.

She stepped into the room, her gaze immediately drawn to the bed in the corner.

"There she is," her father said.

Without realizing she was holding it, Leah released a long breath and felt a genuine smile take hold of her mouth.

He was alive. Moreover, he looked it.

She crossed the room and kissed her father's cheek. "Daddy."

He gazed at her steadily as she drew back. "Gave you and your sister a bit of a scare there, didn't I?"

Leah half laughed, afraid a sob would follow quickly on its heels after all that had transpired in the past twenty-four hours. "Yes, I guess you could say that."

She looked at him, really looked at him.

More than the color had returned to his cheeks. He looked better in general than he had in a long, long time. Well, despite that he was lying in bed with tubes snaking in and out of him. His eyes were more alert. His face looked less drawn.

And that grin...

"Lord save us all from that charming grin," she whispered. It was what her mother used to say about Judge Jonathon Dubois whenever he wanted something and turned on the charisma full throttle to get it.

Her father chuckled softly then a somber expression fell over his face. He reached for her hand and squeezed. "I'm sorry that this had to happen so soon after losing your mother, Leah."

She searched his face, unable to believe what he was saying. He'd just gone through what was probably the most frightening moment of his life and he was thinking about her. "You're apologizing to me? Daddy, the one you need to be apologizing to is yourself."

He blinked at her.

Leah battled against the demons haunting her and said softly, "You have no idea how worried Rachel and I have been about you since Mom died...." She trailed off, holding his hand in both of hers, her thumb skimming over his dry skin. "I'm just glad you decided to fight."

His grip on her hands tightened. "You didn't think it would be that easy to get rid of me, did you?"

She laughed softly.

"Now I want to hear about what's going on with you."

She squinted at him.

"I know something's going on, Leah. You were always as good at hiding things as Patricia was. And that's not good at all."

She smiled sadly at that.

"Is this about Dan?"

She tugged her hands from his and reached for the carafe of ice chips on the table next to the bed. "In some ways, yes."

"You're not going through with the reconciliation."

It was more of a statement than a question. Leah watched him as she tried to spoon-feed him some of the ice chips. He accepted one spoonful but refused the next.

"I'm not an invalid, Leah," he chastised softly.

She sighed as she put the carafe back on the table. "No, Dan and I aren't going to reconcile. I just know we shouldn't be together. Only I haven't told him yet."

She felt her father's gaze on her face.

"You shouldn't have to tell him, Lee. It's been written there on your face for a long time now. Since even before you divorced him."

Her gaze flew to his.

He smiled at her as he smoothed his folded blankets across his hips. "What, you didn't think I got to be a judge by being stupid, do you? I could see you didn't love him, Leah. Could see it from the beginning, if you want to know the truth."

"But you treated Dan like a son."

He nodded. "Yes, I did. But how I felt about Dan and how you feel about Dan are two different things. For one thing, I don't have to share a bed with him. You do."

Leah felt her face go hot.

Her father turned his head to stare at the ceiling, wearing what she called his judge's face. Pensive, forbidding and wise. "Three months ago when you told me you were thinking about reconciling with Dan I wanted to impose a sentence on you of one month in your room."

Leah rubbed her hands against the material of her

slacks, remembering that's how he used to dole out punishment. Missed a homework assignment? A sentence of one week doing dinner dishes. Grades dropped below an "A"? A one-month sentence of no television and outings only on the weekends, with no opportunity for parole.

But nothing, nothing, ever got in the way of their Saturday afternoon dance sessions. Her father would power up his old Vitrola and dust off his old jazz and blues LPs and she, Rachel and their mother would take turns letting Jonathon Dubois Astair twirl them from the study out into the foyer and back again.

Her father cleared his throat. "While you might not think I knew much about what was going on in your life or Rachel's life beyond your grades and disciplining you, I did know you were having an affair when you finally decided to end things with Dan."

Leah's throat grew tight. She had tried so hard to keep the information quiet. Something that had been easy to do because she and J.T. had met on the sly.

Little had she known that the secrecy hadn't been because he didn't want more than sex from her. It had been because he was on the run.

And, as it was turning out, everybody had known about the affair anyway.

"Who is he?"

Not who was he, but who *is* he.

"Do I know him?"

"Actually, you met him once. A long, long time ago."

"Ah," he said, shifting in the bed and wincing when his chest must have pulled tight. "That Westwood boy."

Leah slowly nodded. "Try not to move too much. You'll pull open your sternum."

He waved her away. "I always thought he was a good boy. I hope he turned into a good man."

Leah eyed him. "You hated him on sight."

"No, I hated that he was the first man I had to share my oldest daughter's love with. I never hated him."

Her eyes filled with tears.

He remained quiet for a long moment, allowing Leah to put herself back together. The problem was that Leah didn't think she'd ever accomplish that task again.

"He's the kind of guy you would never have approved of my marrying," she whispered.

His eyes shifted to stare into hers. "If you'll remember correctly, I didn't approve of your marrying Dan."

"Because of my age."

"No...because you didn't love him."

Leah blinked quickly.

"Oh, you thought you did. But your mom and I knew that you didn't." He searched her face. "This Westwood boy...you love him?"

She stared down at her hands and nodded.

"So what's wrong, then?"

Leah had never talked to her father in such a casual way about her love life. That had always been her mom's job. And, oh, how she missed Patricia's no-nonsense advice.

She gazed into her father's eyes and felt a dam give way in her chest. "Oh, Daddy. Everything's such a mess. Sami hates him. Josh is in some kind of trouble that I won't go into detail about now.... Everything looks so impossible."

His features stilled and she was afraid he'd pulled something loose. She began to lean forward to check when he said, "Did I ever tell you about the time I went to Las Vegas? The week before I married your mother?"

Leah shook her head, trying to focus on his words.

"No, of course, I didn't. Because you wouldn't have been ready to hear it."

Then he proceeded to tell her a story that made her eyes bug out of her head and her heartbeat quicken with hope.

When he finished, he reached out his hand and

touched the side of her face. "Nothing's impossible, Leah. All you have to do is believe...."

THE ROAD UNDER J.T.'S BIKE felt bumpy and uneven, seeming to mirror his life as the Harley's motor droned on down the road, away from Leah, away from all that was warm and familiar, away from all that was important to him. The sun was at his back and he'd been riding for the past twelve hours, stopping only for gas and coffee and a roll that wasn't sitting well in his stomach.

He thought about Leah back at home alone. He thought about her worrying about her father, how she was going to repair her relationship with her daughter. And he thought about her hurting because of him.

His fingers tightened on the handgrips, his desire to bring everything to a conclusion tempting him to speed toward his goal. It took every ounce of willpower he had not to push the powerful engine to its limit. But the last thing he needed was to attract the attention of the local authorities. He might wind up in some small-town jail where Leah wouldn't be able to spring him before the police figured out who he was.

He yearned to pull off to the side of the road and call her. If just to hear her voice. But he wouldn't allow himself the selfish luxury. She'd been right in her concerns. If he couldn't clear his name, make things right in his life, or if ended up in prison, everything between him and her would be…well, there would no longer be anything between them. He knew all too intimately what it was like to live on the run and he'd never do that to Leah. And he wouldn't have her wait for him while he rotted away in a prison cell.

It seemed ironic, somehow, that running had chased him to where he wanted to be, and being there now made it imperative that he go back and clean up a mess he should have taken care of long ago.

He thought about the money in his seat compartment. Money he'd accumulated over the years and tucked away, having no use for it beyond his day-to-day living expenses. It was enough to make the attorney he'd used all those years ago salivate.

But after ten years, had the evidence against the sheriff been buried along with the sheriff's young, faithless wife? Was his trip back to the past too long in coming?

J.T. set his jaw and squinted off into the horizon. However it turned out, he had to do this. Had to make things right. Not just for him, but for Leah.

THREE DAYS HAD PASSED SINCE J.T. had left. Three days filled with classes, house chores and trips back and forth to the hospital and her father's house to keep things running. Rachel was so busy with her wedding arrangements that Leah hadn't had the heart to ask her to pitch in more .than she already was.

Besides, being busy helped keep her mind off J.T. and where he was. And how he was doing.

It also kept her from having that talk with her sulky daughter.

Ever since Dan had dropped her off the day before last, she and Sami had lived in the same house but had barely spoken two words to each other at a time. They ate breakfast and dinner together, even sat watching television at night, but the extent of their verbal interaction was one-word questions and answers. From time to time she thought she saw her daughter wearing a remorseful expression. But then she'd look again and find Sami glaring at her as if everything in her life stank and Leah was completely to blame.

What did emerge interesting was that Sami didn't appear to be interacting with her father much now, either.

Leah sat at her kitchen desk and sealed the last of the envelopes that held the payment for her monthly bills. She sat back, listening to the sound of a sitcom in the family room, then glanced at the clock. Just after eight.

Now was as good a time as any to put an end to the cold war.

She got up, gathered her purse and jacket, then went to stand in the doorway to the family room.

"I'm going out for a while," she told her daughter, who sat on the couch, her gaze glued to the television set.

"Are you going to see *him?*"

Leah figured it was a good thing she was so far away from her daughter or she might have been grounded for life. That was saying a lot.

"'Him' as in J.T.? No." She didn't think it a good idea to let Sami know he wasn't in town lest she pray to some unknown God that he not return. "I'm going to see your father."

Interesting. She had expected Sami to be happy with the news. Instead her expression grew sulkier.

She shrugged into her lightweight jacket. "I should be back by ten. If you need anything, call my cell."

"I won't need anything."

No, Leah thought, she probably believed she didn't. But she would. And when that time came, Leah would be there for her daughter. Now and always.

And part of that responsibility meant she had to set things straight with Sami's father right now.

17

LEAH HAD BEEN DREADING THIS conversation with her ex-husband since she'd realized she was going to have it. But now that she stood outside the door to Dan's condo, she was all right with it.

Her heart belonged to J.T. It was as simple and as complicated as that.

The past few days had given her time to think about what her dad had said. Could he be right that she had never really loved Dan? That things had gone so fast that she'd never stopped to examine her feelings for a man she'd been married to for eleven years? Oh, she'd come to love him. But in love? Had she ever been truly in love with him? Or had Josh Westwood stolen her heart long ago and she'd no longer had it to give when she'd met Dan?

Of course, that was neither here nor there now. All that remained was to close old doors and, she hoped, open new ones.

Speaking of doors, she raised her hand to knock on the steel door of Dan's condo. She'd only ever seen the outside of the apartment when she dropped Sami off or picked her up. She now found that odd.

The door opened and Dan stared at her as if she was the last person he expected to see. And she probably was, considering.

She shrugged inside her coat. "Sorry. I probably really should have called first...."

Dan let go of the doorknob and straightened. He still had on his dress slacks and pressed white shirt, but the tie was gone and his sleeves were rolled up to his elbows. The sight was strangely familiar. "Yes, Leah, you probably should have called."

She grimaced, looking back at where a couple was heading to a neighboring condo.

"Can I talk to you for a minute?" she asked.

He looked behind him and only then did Leah catch on that he wasn't alone.

The realization caught her unawares.

"It won't take long," she said, purposefully stepping past him and into the condo.

She hadn't known what she'd expected when she entered, but it certainly wasn't what she was seeing. Dan had taken so little when he'd left their house she'd thought he'd probably gone bachelor mode with his new place. Instead she was confronted with ultrafeminine Art Deco décor complete with black and pink female masks bearing white feathers on the wall, and a glossy black coffee table in front of white leather furniture.

She blinked several times as a woman came out of what presumably was the kitchen, carrying a tray of what looked like crackers and soup.

The woman appeared as shocked as Leah felt.

Then again, Leah thought she came out the winner in any shock contest simply because the woman was at least eight months pregnant.

"Oh…" she whispered.

Dan was still holding the door open. He quickly closed it then came to stand in front of Leah, tucking his shirt into his pants as he went. Funny, she hadn't noticed how thick he was getting around the middle. And was his light brown hair thinning, or was it just her?

"I'm glad you stopped by, Leah, because I've been meaning to talk to you, too."

Leah looked around him to the woman who still stood holding the tray. She began to reach out to shake the woman's hand, then settled on a wave instead. "Hi, I'm Leah."

She didn't say Burger lest it sound like she was laying claim to Dan. And that's not what she'd come here to do no matter her stunned reaction at seeing the other woman.

"I know. It's finally nice to meet you. I'm Glenda."

Leah smiled, shock still winning out over the other emotions trying to push past it. "I'd like to say it's finally nice to meet you, Glenda, but, well, I'm afraid I didn't know you existed."

Dan turned and said something to Glenda then ushered her back into the kitchen. Glenda caught Leah's gaze before she completely disappeared. "It was nice meeting you, Leah."

Dan closed the kitchen door after the other woman then turned to face her.

"Well," Leah said, wondering if her eyes were as wide as they felt. She gestured toward the kitchen, then motioned with her hands around her belly. "Yours?"

Dan didn't appear to understand.

"The baby she's carrying," Leah clarified. "Is it yours?"

"Oh." Dan's face reddened and as he ran his hand through his hair she realized it *was* thinning.

Shouldn't she have noticed these things about him? How had she not noticed?

"Yes. Yes, it is."

Leah looked around her, but wasn't really registering anything. "How long have you two been... seeing each other?"

There wasn't one piece of furniture in the place that indicated a life before Glenda. Not a recliner, not an expensive stereo center, nothing.

"Two years."

Leah stared at her ex-husband again. Two years… That would make it nearly eight months before her initial affair with J.T. Eight months before she'd even thought about asking Dan for a divorce.

She looked down to find she had her hands stuffed deep into the pockets of her overcoat. "Thanks for telling me the truth." She stretched her neck. "Although life would probably have been a whole hell of a lot easier had you told me a little sooner."

She began walking toward the door.

"Wait," Dan said on a sigh.

Leah paused but didn't turn back around.

"What was it you came here to talk to me about?"

She laughed softly, humorlessly. "I came here to tell you I was calling off the reconciliation." She slowly turned back around. "You weren't really going to move back into the house, were you?"

He ran a hand over his face. "Actually, yes, I was."

"You and—" she motioned toward the kitchen "—Glenda were on the outs?"

"No. I was going to let her have the condo."

Leah nodded as if she understood, but she slowly changed to shaking her head because what she was hearing didn't make any sense at all. "Why?"

"Because I love you."

Leah winced. She'd always taken his words at face value before, never having had cause not to doubt them. But now…well, now she wondered how many of his words she should have questioned.

He sighed heavily. "Okay, I want us to get back together because I lost a lot of money in the stock market over the past year and I can't afford both the alimony and child support payments in addition to the kid that's on the way."

"So you were going to reconcile with me so you could make your monthly budget.…" Leah prompted.

"That and I've been asked to run for the seat your father will vacate when he wins his bid for Ohio Supreme Court."

Leah stepped toward the white leather couch. "Do you mind if I sit down for a minute? I think I'm feeling a little sick."

He rushed to her side and helped her sit, then took the chair across from her.

Leah sat for long moments trying to absorb everything. Then the reason for her daughter's sullen mood occurred to her. "I take it Sami met Glenda Monday night?"

"No. She met Glenda a year ago. But because of the pregnancy, over the past several months I've made sure the two of them haven't crossed paths." He frowned. "But Monday night we finally told her.

She wasn't too pleased to find out she was going to be having a little sister or brother in a couple of weeks.''

Nine months pregnant. Glenda was nine months pregnant.

Leah nodded. Of course, Sami hadn't been happy. A mammoth monkey wrench the size of her father's pregnant girlfriend had been thrown into her plans to get her parents back together.

She let out a short burst of air that sounded somewhere between a laugh and a snort.

"What's so funny?" Dan asked.

Leah shook her head. "What's the matter with all of us? Not just you and me, and J.T. and Glenda, but the world at large? Why are we always rationalizing ourselves into doing things we would otherwise never do?" She pulled her hands out of her pockets and rested her face against them. "Is that what life is about? Settling? I should settle for you because there's currently nothing else going on in my life and, well gee, Sami would like to have her father living back in the house, and gee, Dan and I have always been such good friends that it shouldn't be that bad...."

She stared at her ex-husband as if he could provide her with an answer, but he looked as dumbstruck as she felt.

She squinted at him. "What about you, Dan?

What about Glenda? Don't you think that baby she's carrying is more important than a bid for a judgeship? Don't you think he or she and Glenda deserve better? I mean, hell, you're obviously living with her and have been for a while. Doesn't she deserve to give her baby a name? Your name?''

She got up from the couch.

''And how much of what you're saying now has to do with J. T. West, Leah?'' he asked, rising as well. ''Or should I say Joshua Thomas Westwood?''

Leah's throat tightened.

''How much of your coming over here tonight to tell me you were calling off the reconciliation has to do with him?''

''Everything and nothing,'' she whispered, her heart giving a sharp lurch.

''Doesn't it concern you in the least that you're putting our daughter at risk every time you see him? Doesn't it bother you that the man killed a woman ten years ago? That he's a fugitive on the run from the law?''

She wasn't surprised he'd uncovered the truth behind J.T.'s identity. Enlisting his help to spring J.T. from jail had guaranteed that he would.

It also meant that local law enforcement knew the truth and had likely contacted the Phoenix authorities.

''No, it doesn't concern me, Dan. And, for what

it's worth, it's none of your damn business anyway."

"Come on, Lee, what do you know about this guy? How do you know he's not the one who broke into your place, sabotaged your car and cut your water pipe?"

Leah stared at him as if he'd grown another head. And in a way he had. Because he'd just revealed himself as the one who had done all three things.

"Why?" she asked. "Why did you do it?"

Dan winced and he rubbed his face in agitation. "What are you talking about?"

"No one knew about all three of those things combined but me and J.T. and the person responsible." She hadn't even known her car had been sabotaged. That bit of news made her head spin.

His shoulders slumped. "I'm sorry, Leah. I really am. I don't know what I was thinking." He shrugged, looking so small in that one moment she actually pitied him. "I guess I thought if you needed me, if there were some reason for you to turn to me…"

Leah sat for a long moment staring at nothing. Then she stepped toward the outer door and opened it. "Glenda?" she said, pretty sure the other woman was listening intently on the other side of the kitchen door. "It was nice meeting you. Good luck with the baby."

Something clattered as if dropped then she heard a quiet, "Thank you."

Leah considered her ex-husband long and hard. She realized that he hadn't done anything unforgivable. Although it might take her some time to be able to extend that forgiveness, she didn't wish him any ill will. "Marry her, Dan, and run for judge. The rest will work itself out. You'll see."

Then she left the condo feeling like the world would somehow never look quite the same again.

WHEN LEAH GOT HOME, the house was quiet. The television and all the lights, aside from the kitchen fan light, had been turned off. She put her purse down on the kitchen counter and shrugged out of her coat. It was only nine o'clock. She usually began asking Sami to get ready for bed at nine and at somewhere around ten the girl might make it as far as her bedroom where she'd talk on the phone for a while or do homework.

Of course, lately her relationship with her daughter had been anything but usual.

She slipped off her shoes then picked them up, dropping them off in her bedroom before continuing on to Sami's closed door. She listened for a moment then knocked. There was no answer. She knocked again.

"Sami, I'm coming in."

She opened the door to find Sami lying on her stomach on her bed with a pair of headphones fastened securely over her ears. Leah could hear the music from where she stood so it was a pretty good bet her daughter hadn't heard her knock or even come in.

She stepped toward the bed and sat down on the side. Sami finally rolled over to stare at her.

"Can I talk to you for a few minutes?" Leah said.

Sami frowned at her.

Leah reached over and lifted the right side of the headphones, the tinny sound of techno music blaring louder. "I said, can I talk to you for a few minutes?"

Sami reluctantly took the headphones off and sat up, pushing herself to the far end of the bed against the headboard.

"What do you want?" her daughter asked with that half pout Leah had gotten far too used to seeing in recent weeks.

Leah cleared her throat, tamping down any ire that began to rise. "I think you and I are overdue for a discussion about your actions the other day."

Sami shifted uncomfortably.

"I've been waiting for an apology, but so far I haven't seen a glimpse of one coming."

Her daughter toyed with the body of her handheld radio.

Leah took it from her, switched it off, then handed it back.

"I'm sorry," Sami said sullenly.

Leah crossed her arms. "Well, that sounded genuine."

Sami sighed and flopped her hands on either side of her. "What do you want me to say? That it was a stupid thing to do and that I didn't mean for Mr. West to get arrested and that…and that…"

Leah waited. "And that…"

Sami launched herself into her arms. "And that whatever you do, please, please don't send me to live with Dad."

Leah supposed that tonight must be her night for shocks.

If someone had told her that her impossible eleven-year-old daughter would be sobbing in her arms within two minutes of her entering the room, she would have told them they were crazy.

Yet here Sami was, her tears soaking through the sleeve of Leah's blouse, her arms wrapped around Leah's arms, pinning them in place.

Leah carefully extracted her right arm and began stroking her daughter's hair. So soft. So clean. How long had it been since she'd been allowed to touch Sami like this? A year? Longer?

"I understand that you, your dad and Glenda had a talk Monday night."

Sami didn't move for a long moment, then she nodded and pulled away to look up into her face. "They're having a baby!"

Leah smiled softly. "Yes, I know. It was, um, kind of hard to miss."

Sami looked down. "Daddy made me promise not to tell you."

"Mmm. I bet he did."

"Are you mad?"

Leah thought long and hard. Was she mad? "No. Surprisingly, I'm not. Shocked, definitely. But not mad." She tucked Sami's hair behind her ear several times before the fine strands stuck there. "Things have been over between your dad and me for a long time, Sami."

Sami crossed her legs and stared at her hands in her lap. "Yes, well, I wish somebody had told me."

Leah gave a soft laugh that earned her a sharp look. "I'm laughing because you're right. I think we would have been a lot better off if we'd all sat down for a good talk a long time ago."

God, she couldn't remember being eleven years old. At Sami's age everything emerged a major Greek drama being played out on the world's stage.

"Do you mind if I ask you a question, Sami?"

Her daughter squinted her blue eyes at her.

"And I want you to be truthful."

Sami sniffled then ran the heel of her hand against her damp nose and nodded.

"Why don't you like J.T.?"

Apparently her daughter must have thought the question would be in regards to her father. She uncrossed her legs and stretched them out, taking an overinterest in aligning her knees. "I don't even know J.T....Mr. West enough to dislike him."

Leah shifted on the bed to sit next to her, stretching out so that her head rested against the pillows and her bare feet next to her daughter's. "Well, then, excuse me, but getting someone arrested because you don't dislike them is a little confusing to me." She patted the pillow next to hers. "Come on, you can tell me."

Sami scooted up then laid her head back against the other pillow, her feet reaching Leah's calves. "I don't know why I did it, Mom. I was just so surprised, you know, when I came out and saw him there. Then he told me that something had happened to grandpa, and he had this...stuff all over his hands and I...freaked."

Leah nodded. "Go on."

Sami looked at her. "That's it."

"That's the reason you accused him of trying to kidnap you."

Sami had the good grace to look guilty. She turned back to stare at her toes. "I don't know."

She shrugged, the movement moving the bed. "I think maybe it was because I got the idea you guys knew each other really, really well, and…it made me feel like the way I feel when Dad's with Glenda."

Leah drew her brows together. That was an interesting way of putting it.

"So you maybe didn't like that I knew J.T. outside of our mother and daughter relationship?"

Another shrug. "I guess so. I mean, it was like it was this big secret, you know. The only difference was that you didn't ask me not to tell Dad about it."

It had felt like a big secret precisely because it had been a big secret.

In all her covert rendezvous with J.T., she'd never once stopped to think that maybe her daughter felt she was being left out.

Of course, there was another factor involved. Leah hadn't exactly been ready to welcome him into her house until just recently.

She rested the top of her head against her daughter's, much the same way she and Rachel did when they indulged in their heart-to-heart talks. "You know that no matter what happens, I love you, don't you, sweetpea?"

Sami rolled her eyes at her use of the old nickname, her ears pinkening. "Please don't call me that, Mom."

"Well? You didn't answer me."

Sami tilted her head down so that her chin nearly plowed into her chest. "Yes, I know."

"And you know that no matter where I am, you're always welcome, right?"

Sami turned to stare at her. "Are we moving?"

Leah elbowed her. "Answer the question."

Sami considered the words for a long moment, then she nodded.

"I want you to promise me something, Sami," she said quietly after a long moment of toenail contemplation passed. "I want you to promise me that no matter how you feel, that you'll always come to me when something's bothering you. I don't want you to keep everything all bottled up anymore. It's not healthy." She nudged her nose into her daughter's hair until she found her ear. "Besides, I'm beginning to worry that all that frowning is going to make you look like an old lady at the ripe old age of eleven."

Sami giggled then nestled down farther into the pillows.

They both lay like that for a while, neither of them saying anything. It had been a long time since Leah had spent an extended amount of time in her daughter's room and she reasoned that it was time to start spending more time there. She looked over the pink little girl décor and wondered if it wasn't also time to update Sami's room to reflect the woman she was going to so very soon become.

Sami's soft voice stirred the hair over her ear. "I love you, Mom."

Leah turned toward her and cuddled her close. "Oh, baby, I love you, too." And if she'd missed her daughter, as well, she wasn't going to say anything. She was just so damned relieved to have her back.

18

THREE WEEKS AND LEAH STILL HADN'T heard from J.T.

She caught herself scratching her arm where she sat taking her Humanities final exam, the test that would determine whether or not she would earn her BBA, bachelor of business administration degree.

The fine hair on the back of her neck stood on end. She slowly looked over her shoulder but didn't see anything other than the regular faces she saw on any other given class day.

Leah sighed and turned her attention back to her exam. The only problem was that every time she blinked, she saw J.T.'s handsome face imprinted everywhere. And with each hour that passed, each second that ticked by, she grew more and more afraid that she might never see him again. Might never again experience his touch. Melt under the power of his kiss.

She swallowed hard and turned the test sheet over although she hadn't finished the first side yet. The ache that had begun the moment she'd watched him ride away had rolled into an ever-present pain that was part of everything she did. She might laugh at a joke her father cracked about his recent surgery. Or trade off-color gossip with Rachel while having lunch. Or enjoy some true quality time with her daughter, Sami. But often were the times when she'd stare wistfully over their shoulders, looking at nothing, hoping for something she was beginning to fear she might never have again.

It had even gotten to the point where merely waiting wasn't doing it for her anymore. But her father and sister had been unable to uncover any more information than she already knew. So last week she'd looked up the phone number of a private investigator in Phoenix and placed a call looking to secure her services to find J.T. Two days later the P.I. had called back to say that she'd found no trace of the man.

Leah had shivered and hung up the phone, her heart pounding in her ears.

She told herself the not knowing was what affected her most. She was prepared for anything that might happen. But not knowing what was going on, not knowing if J.T. had headed for points unknown, again on his own, again on the run, was what turned her inside out.

But she knew that wasn't true. What was eating her alive was not knowing how J.T. was doing.

If he, indeed, had discovered there was no way to clear his name, and had decided that living life on the lam was his only option, she at least wanted to know that. Wanted to hear his voice one last time before she resigned herself to the fact that she'd never see him again.

She longed for something, anything, other than this infernal nothingness.

Two hours later the time bell rang, signaling the period allotted for the final was over.

Leah blinked then slowly closed her exam booklet, barely remembering a single thing she'd done in the past hundred and twenty minutes. She passed the test forward then gathered her class material and purse and headed for the door.

It seemed odd for some reason that the sun should be shining when she emerged from the underground classrooms of the University of Toledo Business College, nicknamed The Bomb Shelter. Strange that the world continued to run at normal speed while the pace of her life seemed to be running in slo-mo. She made her way to her car, thinking of plans she'd made to fill her day.

Then she got into the car and instead of driving home, she headed to the house outside of town that J.T. had worked on before he left. The house they had made love both inside and outside of.

She slowed on the two-lane route outside the

house and squinted at the two-story Victorian in the bright midday sun. Apparently the owners had taken possession and she watched as a young woman tried to catch a toddler running away from her on the front lawn, sans diaper, blond curls blowing in the late spring wind, while another older child played with a cocker spaniel a few feet away.

Leah smiled regretfully. Could that have been her with J.T.'s children? If things had worked out differently? If his father hadn't moved after that summer so long ago, taking J.T. to a different place and leaving her to move on to marry Dan?

Her hand dropped to her stomach. She had secretly hoped that she had become pregnant as a result of their one irresponsible night of making love without protection. But she'd gotten her period a week and a half ago and even that hope had been crushed.

Of course, poor Sami likely would have run away had her mother gotten pregnant so soon after her father had had another child.

Leah dropped back against the headrest. Dan had gotten himself a little boy. She had taken Sami to the hospital to try and ease her into accepting her half sibling, not expecting to be drawn to the child herself. Oh, no, she harbored no feelings either way for her ex-husband. She certainly knew they could never be more than Sami's parents. But there was something about the…promise in the new family that made her heart pulse and her body yearn for something she preferred to leave unnamed.

Surprisingly, the instant Sami had gazed through the nursery window at her little brother, it was love at first sight. Leah doubted her daughter would ever share the closeness with her father that Leah wished for—or was that a father-daughter thing? While Leah adored her own Dad, he wasn't her friend. It had always been her mother she had run to. Anyway, she was glad Sami was learning to forge a path for herself in both families that didn't include constantly conspiring to reunite her parents.

Dan and Glenda were set to get married in a simple ceremony next week, and Sami was going to be the maid of honor.

"Nothing's impossible, Leah. All you have to do is believe."

She recalled her father's words to her that first day following his surgery.

She also recalled the story he'd told her.

Leah shifted in the leather seat and stared out at the road ahead of her trying to imagine her father as she'd never seen him before. Trying to see him at twenty-three, a week before he was to marry a woman he'd always loved, her mother. Tried to envision him wearing his best suit and accepting his friends' offer to fly him to Las Vegas for one last outing as a bachelor.

She wasn't surprised that gambling hadn't been his thing, while his three friends had spent the entire weekend at the betting tables.

She *had been* surprised that he'd fallen for a showgirl whose heel had broken during her first show and who had fallen from the stage and into his lap where he'd sat in the front row.

He'd said he'd tried to reason away his attraction to the young woman. Tried to remind himself that he was getting married in a week to the woman he loved. But his heart refused to hear what his mind was trying to tell it and he'd spent the whole three days with her, exploring feelings he'd never experienced before. An excitement, a shimmering lightness that had both drawn him in and scared him to death.

And it had been that fear, and his own sense of duty to his bride back home, that had made him get on that plane Sunday night and vehemently vow never to look back.

The problem was that he had looked back. Often. He'd find himself lying in bed late at night next to his wife and wonder what had happened to that beautiful woman who had taken his breath and a piece of his heart away during that fateful weekend.

No, he'd never thought about trying to contact her.

Until his wife had died and his life had gaped empty and dark.

"I didn't believe it could work. I didn't believe that the life I had planned out for myself, my career in law, would go anywhere if I married a showgirl," he'd told Leah as he'd lain in that hospital bed, having come as close to death as one person could get. "And while I don't regret my life with your mother or my life with you girls, I sometimes wonder what would have happened if I hadn't gotten back on that plane...."

Leah blinked then turned her head to glance at the young mother in front of the house to her right. The woman used her hand to shield her eyes from the sun, having spotted the lone car on the road and the woman looking in her direction. Leah raised her head from the rest, gave a small wave then finally put the car into gear and headed for home.

If only she didn't feel like she was getting on her own plane of sorts and leaving something behind her.

LATER THAT NIGHT, after dinner had been eaten, chores seen to, and after Sami had gone up to finish some homework before going to bed, Leah ticked yet another day without J.T. off her mental calendar.

Her movements were lethargic as she put away the last of the dishes from the dishwasher then checked for the things she would need for breakfast in the morning and for Sami's lunch.

No bread.

She leaned against the counter, staring blankly into the empty bread box, trying hard not to think about how she felt just as hollow.

And trying not to think about how it had been a bread run that had brought J.T. back into her life.

She closed the bread box door with a dull, tinny click. Maybe she'd just give Sami money to buy lunch at school tomorrow.

And toast in the morning?

She turned and took a plastic pack of frozen English muffins out of the freezer, the bag clunking against the countertop.

Her shoulders slumped as she slid onto the stool on the other side of the island counter and propped her head in her hands. It was always this time of day that did her in. When night fell and the day was done and there were no more mundane activities with which to fill her time. More often than not she ended up sleeping on the couch in the family room, rather than enduring the torture of climbing into that huge bed she swore still smelled like J.T. alone no matter how many times she changed the sheets.

It was times like now that the self-pity monster

she strained to hold at bay cracked through her barrier and ran wild, pointing out that everything seemed to be working out for everyone else. Rachel was getting married to a wonderful man in less than a month. Her father was well on the road to recovery and looked better than ever. Sami's grades had improved and she suspected she had a crush on a boy at school. Even Dan was marrying a woman Leah hadn't even known existed a short time ago. A woman who had just given birth to his child.

And she…

And she moved through the days of her life on automatic pilot, finishing school, pushing forward with her plans to open the satellite shop of Women Only in a little over two months, taking care of and nurturing her daughter.

And crying at the kitchen counter over something as stupid as a loaf of bread.

"One thing I'll never be able to handle is the sight of a beautiful woman crying."

Leah's head jerked up and she hiccuped, running her fingers over her face to wipe away the dampness. The wholly male, utterly intoxicating voice had sounded quietly from behind her.

And she didn't dare turn around for fear that she'd discover it was nothing more than her imagination.

Something brushed against her hair and she shivered, her eyes drifting closed and a groan crowding her throat.

"I'd like to promise that you'll never have reason again to cry, but I don't think I can," the voice continued, so close to her ear she started trembling. "What I can promise is that your tears will never again be over worrying about me."

Oh, God, J.T.....

Leah swung around and threw herself at the man she'd been so worried about, the man she'd missed like an amputated limb, the man who filled her heart and haunted her dreams, clutching him tightly to her chest as if she might never let him go.

And she never intended to. Not again. Not ever.

J.T. chuckled softly as he edged his thumb under her chin and lifted her face. Her pulse skittered and an all too familiar melting sensation took hold of her body as she stared into those sweet golden brown eyes.

He'd come back to her.

Then he was kissing her.

Kissing her so deeply, so thoroughly, so passionately that Leah's heart felt like it was breaking all over again. In that instant she knew that what her father had told her at the hospital following his surgery was right. Love, true love, could never be denied or ignored. It thrived and breathed with a life of its own.

And she loved J.T. with everything that she was and would ever be.

She framed his face in her hands and pulled back. His features were a very welcome blur and she blinked rapidly to bring him back into focus. She knew a moment of panic. Could he have come to say goodbye one last time?

His smile was soft and loving and made her insides feel like water. "Are you back? For…good?"

He ran the backs of his fingertips over her cheek as if unable to believe he was touching her again. He nodded. "I'm back…for good."

Leah melted into his embrace again, instantly forgetting the long, unrelenting torment of the past three weeks. Pushing aside the memory of her cold, empty bed and all the doubts and fears that had clung to her like so many layers of unwanted clothing.

"What happened?" she barely dared to whisper. "Is it over?"

"It's over, baby. It's over."

She pulled back to search his face.

He took her hand and tugged her to her feet. "Sheriff Dumont is safely behind bars, where he belongs."

She'd lived with the fear of losing him for so long, she couldn't bring herself to believe it. "But…how?"

He kissed the top of her head. "It seems our un-friendly sheriff married another young wife. And when things started turning sour a year and a half ago, she began fearing for her life. With good reason. It seems Dumont figured he got away with it the first time, the second time should be a piece of cake. But the Arizona District Attorney's Office wouldn't act on the second wife's fears. At least until I came back onto the scene. I was the one last cog needed to set the whole machine into motion.

"I helped set up the sting with the Phoenix Police Department's Homicide Division, and see it through, the end result being a video tape with Dumont not only outlining his plans to do away with his new wife, but giving a detailed description on how he got rid of his first." His hands skimmed down her back and he pressed her to him, making her aware of every inch of his body and just how much he wanted her on every level, made apparent by the thick ridge behind his zipper that pressed into her quivering belly. "I wasn't going to tell you now, but I brought the sheriff's young wife to Toledo with me. Would you mind giving her a job at your new shop?"

An image of J.T. in bed with the sheriff's first wife singed her mind.

He grinned down at her. "Baby, you never have anything to worry about in that department. I was born to love you. And I'll die loving you." He kissed her, his mouth conveying the truth in his words. "There's no one else in this world for me but you."

Leah's entire body swelled with heat and love.

"And I'm going to do my best to be all I can for you. I'll be there for Sami. I'm going to keep working, but I'm also going to get that mechanical engineering degree I always meant to—"

"Mom, I..."

Sami.

Leah told herself she should pull away to address her daughter. But she couldn't seem to let go of J.T. as she looked at Sami where she had just entered the room. The eleven-year-old stood staring at the two of them in confusion.

Leah knew a fear that J.T.'s return would set back the painstaking progress she'd made with Sami.

Instead Sami stepped over to her side, and looked up at J.T. "I'm glad you're back. Maybe now my mom won't spend every night crying."

And just like that Leah believed. She believed that J.T. was back for good. She believed that her daughter had begun to accept her as a person and not just a mother. And she began to believe that they, the three of them, had the makings of a family so full of promise she thought her heart might burst.

Epilogue

One month later...

RACHEL HAD TO BE THE PRETTIEST bride Leah had
ever laid eyes on. However, she was in contention
for the title of happiest. The latter role would have
to go to herself, because the day after J.T. had rolled
back into town on his Harley, he'd whisked her to
the county courthouse and within an hour she had
become Mrs. Joshua Thomas Westwood, something
it seemed she had waited a lifetime for.

Jonathon Dubois had just knocked on the door to
let his daughters know that he was waiting in the
hall, ready to give his youngest daughter away to
her groom.

Rachel dropped her voice, although Leah was
pretty sure nothing could penetrate the thick wood
and stone room.

"I can't believe Daddy's rescinding his bid for
Ohio Supreme Court Judge and leaving for Vegas
tomorrow," Rachel said as she straightened her veil

in the cheval mirror in the antechamber of St. Joseph's Church. "I mean, what is he thinking?"

Leah glanced at her sister's reflection and tugged the veil back to its rightful position. "He's not. He's feeling." She hugged her sister from behind. "Which is exactly what you should be doing instead of thinking about Daddy's plans right now."

Rachel's smile could have easy rivaled all the lights in Paris. "You're right."

Leah smoothed her hands down her sister's silky smooth arms, envying the flawlessness of her skin. "I'm always right."

The two sisters smiled at each other for a long moment in the mirror, enjoying the moment, this moment, right before Rachel was due to marry the man she loved, knowing that with the words "I do" so much would change.

"Do you think he'll find her?" Rachel asked.

Leah didn't have to ask who she was talking about. She knew that their father was the "he" and the "her" was the woman, the young showgirl he'd had that premarital fling with so long ago and hadn't gotten out of his heart since.

"I don't know. But I think it's a good thing that he's trying."

Rachel nodded, her features clouding over.

Leah searched her sister's face. "What's wrong?"

She blinked, remaining silent for a heartbeat before slowly shrugging. "I don't know.... I guess today, when I'm wishing with all my heart that Mom were here, it's difficult to think of Dad with anyone else."

Leah idly touched the lines of flowery lace interwoven with freshwater pearls on the bodice of her sister's dress. "I know."

The yards of fabric that were Rachel's skirts rustled as she turned to face Leah. "What do you think she'd say, Lee? You know, if she were here right now?"

Leah smiled as she picked up the bouquet of peach-colored roses and baby's breath and handed it to her sister. "Oh, probably that you wouldn't want to keep that very handsome groom of yours waiting."

Rachel rose to her feet, taking Leah's breath away with the picture she made.

Leah hugged her and whispered, "I know exactly what she'd say, Rachel. She'd tell you to go out there and marry that man of yours and live every moment of your life to the fullest."

"Do you think?"

Leah nodded. "I know."

Her sister hugged her again then turned to head for the door. She stopped halfway there and looked at her over her shoulder. "Oh, by the way. That big box with the Women Only wrapping paper I saw in your car this morning had better be for me.''

Leah stood back and smiled, then smoothed the red silk of her dress before going out to join her adored and adoring husband and her daughter in the first pew, wondering why more people didn't lead their lives with their hearts and forget about their heads.

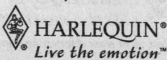

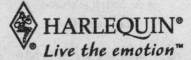

**Experience two super-sexy tales
from national bestselling author**

A collector's size volume
of HOT summer reading!

Two extraordinary women explore their deepest romantic desires
in Mallory's famously sensual novels, *Love Game* and *Love Play*.

Catch the sizzle…in May 2004!

"Ms. Rush provides an intense and outrageously sexy tale…"
—*Romantic Times*

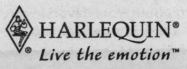

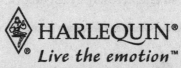

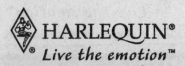